To Cynthia

Hope you enjoy!

Roof Alexander

ALLWEAREIS
PUBLISHING

This book is a work of fiction. Names, characters, places, and incidents are products of the author's imagination or are used fictitiously. Any resemblance to actual events, locales, or persons, living or dead, is entirely coincidental.

Copyright © 2014 by Roof Alexander
First edition
All rights reserved

Allweareis Publishing
Brooklyn, NY
www.roofalexander.com

ISBN-13: 978-0615989891
ISBN-10: 0615989896

For the inspiration of these pages
For the greatest *living* poet
TQ

THE ARROGANCE OF USELESSNESS

ROOF ALEXANDER

"I have no money, no resources, no hopes. I am the happiest man alive."

Henry Miller

PROLOGUE

The rain had been falling for three straight nights. Refuge was sought in the tavern. Social interaction needed to prove their existence otherwise. He sat at the bar, tossing a coin into the air in front of his face. His goal, benevolence, his methods, masochistic. When this didn't draw the audience he needed for the experiment, the man began to follow the toss with a catch-and-slap against the wooden bar-top. He then would cup his hand over the coin and peek under the shelter to reveal the result in his mind only.

"Heads or tails?" The coin slapped down on the bar.

"The trials of fate." The coin flipped into the air.

"The willingness to let the universe choose our life." The coin slapped down on the bar.

"Gravity and money working together." The coin flipped into the air.

"Two unsubstantiated theories to prove the arrogance of the afterlife." The coin slapped down on the bar.

Those around him had begun to point and whisper about the current stage performance. Once the buffoon had the audience at their peak attention, he asked for an assistant.

"Heads or tails?" The coin flipped into the air.

"Life or death?" The coin slapped down on the bar.

His question, a riddle, his answer, imponderable.

The assistant, seemingly a fool, for fear saves lives, pride procreates, but more than anything, indifference murders.

The buffoon then pulled a capsule from the lint of his pocket, and placed it on display for the audience. "United States Navy Seal issue suicide pill. My father had two of these, now there is only one. My assistant and I will flip for the privilege to enter purgatory with life still strong on our shoulders. Choose the side correctly, take the medicine."

The riddle was now apparent to the assistant and to the audience. There was doubt in the air, clucking of justified challenges. The capsule was over three decades old and no one in the room including the heretic held knowledge of such expiration dates. "It is true that only fate knows what fate will give. All I know is, one toss, one guess, and one pill. Then we all shall see."

"Let me see the coin?" The assistant asked as if asking for just a little more time. They didn't want to die, not yet, not till they figured out how to deal with not existing. All those wasted years in church, in philosophy classes, inside of inspirational books, and they still weren't sure what color darkness would be, what blindness and deafness felt like. Nothing went wrong. It's just what happens every time.

The speaker of the house flipped the coin up to the assistant. "Use your own coin. Use anyone else's coin. Fate isn't a trick. Life isn't forever, and death is a much greater mystery than this pill on the bar."

The assistant pulled out his own quarter. He slammed the coin down, replicating the movements of what had been before. Looking down upon the world, observing over the millions of years how they keep copying each other until someone accidentally gets it right. This was the only reason to let them keep trying.

"I'll take tails!" He said, but had no plans on taking the suicide capsule. He had already planned to beat the buffoon to a bloody pulp if the coin landed on tails. "Is this what you really want?"

The audience held their breath.

The buffoon said nothing. He simply took the quarter and flipped it into the air. As the turning coin hit its peak and began to come back down the bartender reached his hand out and snatched it out of the air. "No one is dying on my shift. Take your non-sense somewhere else." Then he put the coin back down on the bar… heads-up.

"Fate has once again intervened." The buffoon looked down at George Washington staring back at him. "Heads. I win." Then he grabbed the capsule, popped it in his mouth, washed it down with the rest of his beer, and said, "Have a great life. It's what you all deserve." Then he walked out of the bar, never to be seen again.

Part 1

there was less and less charcoal smell in the air every day...

Day 12,299

At some point I would have to wake up. It was most likely around noon. At some point I would have to wake up. It was most likely around 12,000 days. My body was paralyzed from defeat, agitated from rectitude, no longer tired, even though I couldn't have slept more than several hours. My mind possessed an itch that usually meant God was deceiving me once again. I was over the line. At some point I would have to go back. It was most likely outside a space called Arcane. At some point I would have to go back. Outside. My eyes opened... It was time to give it another shot. At some point I really did have to wake up. I just couldn't figure out how to get back there.

My two-room hovel held the time like a solar oven. After 12,000 days it was easy to figure out that it must have been around noon. The sweat. The wet dust. The sparkling dust. But, secretly, I'm not that perceptive, or convicted for that matter, and in the most pathetic way, the slam of my iron mailbox was one of the two higher powers that put me back into life on most days. The mail lady was meticulously time sensitive, punctual to my distorted reality. There were a few precious seconds before she got away, so I couldn't brush my teeth, clear out my eye crust, or remove other splinters under the surface of my mirrors. I went straight for the door, opened it, and found no mail lady. I wasn't really in love with her, but she left me things, postal necessities and other random gifts. Almost no one else did that. There was a stack of advertisements and banana peel coupons. I figured it out. It must have been one of the Wednesdays. Coupon Wednesday! On top of the stack was a mini-billboard, laminated, almost plastic picture of a man dipping his lady on a dance floor while surrounded by a million deliriously happy people. The couple had these smiles that immediately made me think of the words *I love you* and *forever* and *hair dye*. You could tell that she really believed in him, in something, I don't know, maybe just in believing. I named them Mr. and Mrs. Calypso or just the Calypsos.

After that one ray of sunshine splashed over my face, everything seemed to be abnormally dusty inside, even more than I felt before. It was as if it had snowed dead skin cells for weeks. I looked into the reflection of a framed photograph. It was of my parents on their one and only vacation in Florida, but it didn't matter, I wasn't looking at them. My eyes seemed to be gray. There were questions that needed to be answered. Questions that only fuzzy reflections could possibly give answers. The last thing I remembered was the rain, the days of rain and finding that capsule. What did I do with it? What happened to the rain? Why did I get up? Why would one leave the warm cozy womb where the world couldn't manipulate their affinity with darkness?

I did have two things to do that day, and it made my gray eyes a little more understandable. First, a pot of coffee. Then I needed to start my essay on happiness; a very simple projection of what it is to be happy. This time I was going to use words and concepts that would make complete sense to the reader. Not like last time. Yes, this time I would be ready. The tools would be ready. My pen and paper were ready. I paced. The shag brown carpet got a beating. I picked up books and read them three minutes at a time, guzzled sugarless coffee, and looked for inspiration in the ceiling. The layers from heaven to hell are of no significance until one has thought deeply about their own limits of sadness. I paced. Then after two hours, I still had an empty piece of paper save the title *Essay on*

Happiness. I pinned Mr. and Mrs. Calypso up on the wall. Goddamn, I loved them. I loved believing in them, believing in believing.

I stacked the rest of the mail close to the trashcan and noticed the postmark from the ad page. It was from a Thursday. Not only was it *not* Wednesday, it could have been days later. I must have been in a fleeting coma, just a reminder to God that nothing could kill me, not even death.

The coma wasn't a big deal. It just essentially meant that I had double or quadruple the work, which was the third thing I had to do that day. Yes, I had three things to do that day, that possible Thursday. It's funny how I could remember lines from books that I read years ago, but couldn't remember what day it was. It reminded me of a line from Proust. "Time passes, and little by little everything that we have spoken in falsehood becomes true." So essentially whatever day I say it is, it eventually becomes. Life could be so easy sometimes.

So, once again, this instance with more vigor and default, I went outside. My car, a dulling red Pontiac Sunbird that I affectionately named Charlie, the girl, not the boy, sat in the driveway wondering if it would ever flash its feathers again. We had grown apart in our views. That is to say, I was becoming more prehistoric as the days added up. The trees were still green, but one could tell the summer was dying. There was less and less charcoal smell in the air every day, the birds mostly chirped with a sigh, and I got up later and later, if at all. I began walking past all the empty driveways toward the bus stop that was about ten southern blocks away. I flapped my fingers along a white picket fence as a child might, and it reminded me that I forgot my work gloves. When I walked back into the house, a picture of my little sister stared back at me. It was strategically placed on the floor beside the telephone. Yeah, why not, I thought, as my hand went to pick up the receiver. When the warm plastic touched my ear I remembered that the line had been cut off for weeks, probably longer.

Just to let you know, the only reason I didn't pay my phone bill was because my ex-employer kept calling for reasons that may or may not have something to do with the many uniforms that seemed to stay in my possession after my last demotion. The bartender uniform must have been worth a few breaths of air, because the homeless sign guy I gave it to thought of it as a new chance on life. It was practically a tuxedo. I told him, "Man lives many lives, sometimes you must die in order to live again. Now take my tuxedo." Boy did he love me after that.

I actually don't think that's why my ex-employer kept calling me, and it certainly wasn't why I didn't pay my phone bill. Truth is, I would love to talk to just about anyone, including my former saint of a boss. He was a nice guy overall. He set me free and he could really hold his own when it came to conversations about vintage Bordeaux.

My ear and the phone formed a layer of sweat. I woke from that ten-minute dream and once again headed off to work. This job was strictly to support my shelter needs. I only had to put in fifteen hours a week for my rent. My landlord and savior, Floyd Stephanopoulos, owned a ton of trees and dirt out in the depths of North Arcane. It was worth a fortune and rising because, just like every mid-size city in this country, we kept watching TV and having babies. We have been pounded out to the edges until ready to be put into the oven. Floyd wasn't sure what to do with the ratty foothill woods while it gained value, so he sent me out there to figure it out. I called it The Sisyphus Project. And even though my obligation was only fifteen hours, I usually spent at least thirty hours out in the wilderness cleaning up wood from the grass, chopping down trees that had it coming, and basically any duty that would hopefully make it easier for developers to build a nice row of houses someday.

Once I was out of my comatose neighborhood, the city streets came fully alive with convinced ambition. There were already several men gathered at the bus stop beside Dairy Queen. My eyes tried to read their minds, but they stared at the sidewalk avoiding my potential assumptions. Every few seconds one of the men would go to the curb and look up the avenue to see if the bus was on its way. This didn't annoy me like it usually did, which meant my mind must have been sufficiently rested. Generally that's what a couple days of sleep does, but in my case it just means that there was some sort of incident in which my body had to shut down. I probably ate some sort of poison mushroom and it didn't work. My incidents could be described as imponderable, so I won't even get into it.

The combination of sweat on my forehead and the sound of cars and birds told me that life was on its way up. The sun was fully out and the blue that surrounded it didn't matter to my fellow bus patrons, but at least they weren't all staring at their watches. One of my best friends was across the street. I may have mentioned him already. He was on the corner of the intersection with a cardboard sign. Ah, the sign! What an amazing invention! A staple of our society and the way it functions. It was a new theory in evolution and survival of the fittest. If one was in trouble with money, or homeless, or a hustler, or just bored, he could make a sign and consequently fight to see another day. If one could sky-write a slogan, that crafty bastard could buy another plane. If one could come up with a clever sign on the corner of Central Avenue and Thomas Street, then one could eat that night.

This particular man, who wore a bartender's tuxedo uniform and had the brightest red and orange streaked hair, was better than most. That day his sign read, CAN YOU PUT A PRICE ON HAPPINESS? I crossed the street while holding out a dollar like it was a surrender flag. I didn't want him to think I was going to take back my tuxedo. We were great friends because when one gives money to a stranger then the taker has to give his ear.

"So, if you could buy happiness, what would be the price?" I asked, now holding my surrender flag like a Chinese finger trap.

He thought for two seconds, neither surprised nor intrigued by the question. "Just a moment's worth or a lifetime?" He had broken sunglasses over his head.

"A moment or lifetime could be one in the same, I don't really understand my own question, and truthfully its purpose might have been just a test for you. As you know, I demand proof in signage."

"Okay." My great friend was convinced that it was definitely a test. I could tell by the way he tugged the one-armed sunglasses down over his eyes.

"Let's just revert to the original. Can you put a price on happiness?" I needed the answer for my essay on happiness since I was still in the research and development phase.

"The answer is…" He put up his hands as if we were at a church revival. "One dollar!"

"Okay, I didn't expect that. Why one dollar?"

"E pluribus unum." He said in a Spanish accent even though the phrase is Latin. The motto from the one dollar bill meant 'out of many, one.'

"Out of many, one?" I asked him just in case he was confused.

"Out of all of the many times money has made me happy… one." He said and pointed to the dollar bill in my hand. "It is the price."

I became famished all of a sudden, so after dropping the dollar bill into his top hat, I walked away from my great friend toward the Dairy Queen window. I ordered a hamburger and a chocolate shake, and then waited with a woman with three small children. The children made wild animal noises. The mother yelled at them to shut-up while she was on her phone but they knew tone more than she ever would, so they became louder upon her request. It was war in the most minuscule form, and just like in the highest form, there would never be a winner.

The bus was coming. I could tell because of the men attempting to form some sort of chronological line. My food came and I had to reach over the mother to get it. "Pardon me Miss." She smiled at me, but not like a friendly smile, like one in front of a hot fudge sundae. Her rotten phony smile made me nauseous. As I left for the bus, the odor of her green gums followed me. I took one sip of the milkshake and it made me gag. It tasted like hot garbage and complacency. The men began to swipe their bus passes. I tried to eat the burger, but something was rancid in between the buns. I opened it to find a black and green tomato. All of the men were sitting and looking out at me. The driver loudly cleared his throat. My jaw clinched up. I threw the food away before boarding the bus and everything became lovely again. "Good morning." I said as if it were my first. The driver recognized my shoes and didn't respond. It wasn't the first time that he had cleared his throat in my presence.

There were a few of us that had nothing to do but stare in wonder at each other. We were individually astounded by the presence of human activity. Some pretended to look out the windows, and some gave in to the distraction of the newspaper. It was all the same crap that helped us get through life more conveniently in a bed of nails sort of way. There were car dealerships, fast food restaurants, pawnshops, banks, and doctor's offices. We were civilized, a sophisticated society, making a run at mediocrity. This road could have been any road in the country. But it wasn't, this was my invention, this little world was no one else's. I alone took responsibility for what existed in my presence.

By the time I got to my stop, every one else had gone away to his or her destinations, except for this one old man that hobbled down toward the door without aim or destiny. It was as if this wasn't his stop, yet he had no choice but to get off. I shuffled behind him. We wore the same shoes. He carried a package that seemed to be too heavy for him. I was ashamed of his desire for balance, and it depressed me to think about it, so I just thought about how many bricks there must be in the world until we were both off the bus. There must be more than I imagined.

Then there was the walk. My work zone was about two miles down some country roads until reaching the woods. That was one of the few beautiful advantages of this area. One could go from strip malls to wilderness in several hundred seconds. Shoes and ice cream to snakes and honeysuckles. I got about a mile and then sat down in the yard of a man I had met some weeks before, probably three, or five, maybe more. The man's name was Willie. I remember I was wearing a New York Yankees baseball cap, something I had once found on the street. Willie was sitting on a metal lawn chair with a twelve pack of PBR beside him in the grass. "Fuck the Yankees!" He said seriously. I stopped to assess the situation, but before thinking I said, "Hey, fuck you man, it's just a hat."

"You wanna beer?" He reached into the box.

"Well, yeah, but still, you just can't say fuck you to someone without a good fight to follow." The beer was warm. Yes, that's right, now I remember; it was the middle of summer, about six weeks before.

It took about eight seconds for the statement to kick in, but when it did, this guy, all 160 pounds in a five and a half foot frame came at me like a madman. I jumped back, "No, no buddy, that was a joke. I don't fight anymore since the accident."

He went back to his chair and never asked about the accident. People like Willie shit and breathe accidents daily. When a person's life turns out to be one continuous accident it is just called life.

Willie and I finished off the 12-pack that day. As I was leaving to go back home he gave me a ladies gold ring without reason. He had been holding it in his non-drinking hand most of the day. He said, "I need to give you something." He put the ring in my hand. "Go pawn it, it'll be cool, you'll get at least sixty bones for it." Maybe it was because I told him I was trying to be a poet and that the only thing I had to do during the day was wait for God to lead me. Maybe he was a disciple or something. Maybe he had used up all of his clout in the pawnshops around town. Most likely it was just that he couldn't bear to get rid of it himself. I eventually pawned the goddamn thing and got exactly sixty dollars for it. Maybe we were friends.

I hadn't been back since then, six weeks worth of accidents under our belts. The house was still, dead, as if no one lived there. I sat under a pine tree and tried to write a poem about a cat and a moon, because that's what his yard made me think of. Don't ask why, I don't even know. My mind got lost in the intense passion for creating, and...

There were sounds of distant eighteen-wheelers when I woke from my nap. The shadow of the tree had moved away from my legs. I went up to Willie's front porch. He had one of those mail slots where the mail falls directly into his house. I took out the sixty dollars and pushed it through the slot. It was a nice gesture from Willie, but he was no disciple, and we weren't friends.

After getting down the road a bit, I began to get desperately paranoid. For some reason, I had the weirdest feeling that he wouldn't get the money, so I went back to investigate. The only thing in view through the slot was a really nice red velvet chair that could have been for a king. Then my mind played a few tricks on me. Did I put money in the slot? Is this even the right house? It really began to bother me, and I wasn't sure why. Even if he didn't get the money, he wouldn't know that there ever was any money, and if he did, I'm sure he would know it was from me. "Yes, that is true." I convinced myself.

Then the door unexpectedly opened. Willie stood there in off-white briefs and blue-striped tube socks. "Holy fuck! I just found sixty bones right here on the floor. Must've dropped out of my pocket last night. Shit, after a case of rotgut, who knows what you'll find the next day. You know?" He laughed and then began a long coughing session until hocking up a greenish snot-ball for the grass. "Yankees!" He greeted me as if I just appeared. "I ain't drinking yet, but you can hang out and watch some TV?"

"No thanks, just saying hi, I have to get some work done today."

"Say, did'ya ever pawn that ring?"

"Nah, gave it to my little sister." I don't know exactly what my purpose was in not telling him. I started to leave, but he started going on about this time he went fishing and how he caught a turtle. As his lips moved in rapid succession, all I could think of was how he was trying to sabotage me and keep me from my duties. My mind became convinced that he knew my purpose, and that he was a destroyer of beauty and anything of artistic worth. My face became flush, and my knees weak. Thoughts of his neck in my hands flashed in my mind. I have to say, writing about it now seems crazy, but it was quite normal then. You just had to be there, the way he just kept rambling on and on about nothing. It was just amazing how redundant he was. I tried to leave.

"Man, Willie, it was great seeing you, but I need to get to work."

"Wait, before you go, I wrote this." He searched over some random papers on an end table. I watched him with contempt from the porch. "The only reason I did it was because all that stuff you were talking about." He handed me a receipt from Wal-Mart. On the back it read:

>THE MOUTH OF THE TOWN
>A CAT TURNED INTO THE WIND
>JUST MOON JARGON

It was brilliant. It was perfect. It was exactly what I wanted to write. I became so angry that instead of fighting him, I kind of ran sideways away from the bastard, swearing to never go back. But I did go back, almost immediately. Only because he yelled, "Is it good?" So I humbly went up to him and gave my honest opinion. "Yes, it is good, it is very fucking good, but let me tell you something, you will never know what it is to be a poet. You just can't sit in a lawn chair all day in the sun while drinking warm beers and listen to strangers talk about the goddamn moon and shit, and expect... Do you not know that you don't have the right to expect a downfall of rocks upon your head just for the action of handing me a page of words!" I was clearly lost. "You cannot expect this! Words aren't shit man. Why would you hand me this, when in an hour you will still have no pants on, it's the same goddamn reason they invented scented candles!" My eyes must have been as big as black balloons.

"Shit man, I was just high, and thought that I'd write my... oh forget it. I'm not trying to be a poet." He sort of crumpled up the receipt.

I could have cracked him over the head for saying that or maybe even given him a hug, like the kind you would give someone if you knew they were about to die or something. "Listen to me, if you want to be a goddamn poet, be one, but understand that it's not about the words. Words are representative of the destiny we fulfill. If you want to be a poet you'll burn that piece of paper right now."

"Burn it?"

"Yeah, while holding it, until it burns your finger tips."

"But I don't want to be a poet." He was obviously lying.

"What's wrong with you man, just fucking give in to it, don't live in fear, if you want to burn your words, then burn them!" I sounded like a preacher, like my dad.

He leaned back against the doorframe, mouth slightly open, unsure of what was going on. Then he reached for a book of matches on the end table and lit the paper. It was more like a party of lawyers than two degenerates that happened to be floating on two different parts of the universe. But the Earth, the fucking ball of disease and standing water stayed right in sync. He thought I was trying to do something other than promote beauty. I could tell by the way he stared at me as the flame touched his fingertips. He let go of the last bit and watched it drift to the planked porch.

"There, you happy?"

I realized after he asked me about happiness that he wasn't a poet after all, and the summer sun made me think of the beach and dried up sweat. I took out my notepad and wrote down his words. "Here, keep'em. I was just joking about that whole poet thing." I took a step off the porch. "I'm going to go move some branches."

Later on, when I was on the Sisyphus Project, I remembered that sixty dollars and smiled. It had been such a confusing day, but that lost sixty dollars was a solid emotion kept. My four-hour shift in the woods was cut slightly short, because my stomach kept reminding me that it hadn't been fed in a few days. There was a bait and tackle shop on the way back to the bus stop that also sold snacks and greatest hit collections on cassette tapes. The store smelled of minnows, mildew, and mothballs, and it always put me in a better mood. It meant that I put in a good day's work and all there was left to do was go home and read, drink, and dream. I just needed a little food to hold me over till the next day. The woman at the register, lovely but bitter, looked over my two sleeves of saltine crackers and the change that gathered beside them. "That'll be a dollar-fifty." She counted off what I owed her and then waved her hand to signify the rest was mine. I chuckled a bit and did the same gesture back toward her, "Thanks, but just keep it for someone who needs it." I tipped my invisible hat to her. "You have an amazing day." After walking out, I stuck my head back in the door. "And keep your head up beautiful lady." I could be a real charmer most of the time.

    I'm not sure what happened. Maybe it was the sun, or the lack of food, or that stressful moment with Willie, but I got dizzy all of a sudden. The humid air engulfed me. I dragged my left hand against the concrete exterior of the shop and shuffled my feet through the gravel until reaching a little grassy hill in the back. The spinning slowed down. There was a cloud of dirt facing me. After getting down a few saltines the spinning finally stopped, and I felt remarkably fresh and satisfied. Life was such a glorious ride. I put the crackers down and pulled out my notebook. I wanted to write a poem to the cashier. She reminded me of my aunt, except shorter, fatter, and more polite. I needed to give this woman a chance to know that life isn't all that bad, and let her know that good things *do* happen to good people. So my pen began to move, out of control, with no regard for rationalism or intellect. The little fatty part below my thumb cramped up, which meant in physiological terms that the poem was done. I read over it with extraordinary pleasure, intrigued by my own madness. She would never understand it, but I guess that really wasn't the point. I put it away and went back to my crackers. I was so damn hungry that I could feel my intestines gnawing at the several crackers already digested. In my panic to eat I hadn't even thought about how great peanut butter would compliment my dinner. And it would be the perfect excuse to go back into the store and give her the poem. This way I wouldn't seem foolish.

As I approached the storefront my fingers scraped the lint in my pockets. I didn't have any more cash. But I did leave a good bit of change on the counter, probably two dollars worth, at least a dollar-fifty. She was reading some pop-culture magazine when I handed her the poem. She looked up from the pages as if I was handing her a bomb threat. She unfolded it and looked at it as if it were blank.

"Don't read it now, wait until I leave, I'm just going to grab a little cheap jar of peanut butter," I rambled out while making my way down the short cluttered aisle. "Just use the change I left before and we'll call it even."

It took her a few seconds to comprehend what was going on. "That money is already in the register."

"Exactly, and don't read the poem until I leave, I'll be completely embarrassed if you do." I had retrieved the only jar they carried, way too big for my needs.

"But it was only seventy-eight cents." Her face had turned sour like she despised me.

"I'm pretty sure it was two, two-fifty, so that just covers this, and seriously, next time I'm here don't mention the poem, it takes a lot out of me to do these little things."

"Sir, I'm sorry but you can't take the peanut butter, it'll be three dollars."

It was no time to argue. I had no ground to stand on. "Well, I have to say that I'm shocked. I thought we had an understanding, a common ground in which very few other humans could ever relate to..." I put the jar down and walked out of the store.

God, when will these daydreams stop! They fly by like seconds in your sleep. I kept waiting for the sane world to catch up with me, but it seemed to be satisfied with its own pace.

I stood outside the bait shop angry with myself. The poem wasn't good enough. Looking around the parking lot and out at the road, it came to me that it must have been Tuesday. Yes, the stillness definitely objectified the day after Monday, no one buying worms and six-packs, just me and the lonely lady with higher morals. She was an exceptional cashier though. What I wanted to do was go back in the store and smash her in the head with a rock, just to make her bleed a little, just to let her know that even *she* leaks like we all do, and all the damn morals and loyalty in the universe couldn't change that. But that was just a fantasy, and honestly I think I was in love with the woman. I pictured her as a possum stuck in the middle of a highway, and knew that the poem wasn't finished. Yes, I'm in love with the pink-lipped possum. She was only a bit older than me, maybe 30, 40, but a nice thick firm body for someone over 40. Yes, I was definitely in love. It was her needy eyes and her modern indifference to anything real. Opposites *do* attract! And I know I said she was *bitter* earlier, but it was really more of a primitive anger, something inherited. So I stomped back in the store, and to tell you the truth it was quite a blur, but I do remember demanding her to dance with me on the basis that she had my change in the register. A tango for seventy-five cents was a deal of a lifetime for her, or maybe it was a salsa, or maybe it was seventy-six cents, either way, I didn't know any dances that constituted rhythm and sequined dresses. We all were fools that day. I also remember the grand finale in which my words were, "Miss, you have been a part of a big elaborate charade that only the dusty store air was witness to." I snatched the poem from her hands and walked off like a stage actor going to the side to wait for my encore. God, I was alive!

 This elongated pick-up truck pulling a sailboat made a big fuss coming into the broken blacktop parking lot. Across the street, a flowerbed screamed at its servant. The green-thumbed lady turned the water-hose on them, and the flowers sat back with casual assuredness, knowing that the beauty they held was temporary and painless. Even the clumps of dirt that my lungs were breathing in couldn't bother me at that moment. I could feel everything. Across the lot I could see the pink lipstick on the ends of several cigarette butts, I could hear the faint sound of a chainsaw, and it was there that I forgot about work, because in my opinion you can't forget something until you remember it, but the point is, I was completely mixed up and for a few seconds I thought that I hadn't worked that day. The tiny scrapes and cuts over my hands told me the truth though. The proof that life had happened.

The bus dropped me off at my stop on Central Avenue, right at Thomas Street. There were all sorts of drunks out on the patio of The Abbey. Several of the drunks were philosophical nemeses of mine when they used to let me in that big phony bar. I tried to stay behind the trees beside the road, but in a way that I would have to be caught. They were all so sure they would see the next day, that they would one day look at a check for a million dollars, that their children would all come out with diamonds in their eyes. Even the ones that weren't slapping their knees and laughing like hyenas were so much in love with the people who were. I bashfully crept away from them with thoughts of... or, more like wishes for their happiness. They all deserve it just for being human, for being born with expectations and tap shoes. I was still young enough to care, that is to say, I was merely an unhealthy child that knew that much more suffering was to come.

My brand new lucidity made me skip through my neighborhood. The streets had a shine of tar and glass. The tree line was a slice of red spectrum, a path to fill one's ribcage. Sometimes when I didn't wake up by the mail lady's presence, I'd sleep till five and then go out and watch everyone coming home from work. The dog walkers, the tennis rackets, kisses from loved ones wrecked me into a lovely war in which I win every time. We're all winners in the land of convinced survival. Someone from above cut the wires from my shoulders and arms and legs, but decided to leave two spools of yarn just for my brain. But I knew that I controlled my mind, and just to prove it to myself, I ordered my feet to run back to The Abbey. And they did.

When they first saw my eyes it was the best thing I'd ever seen. "Just dropping by to say hi." My hand did a sort of semi-circle. "I'm not drinking anymore, so I would say that I generally just don't like to hang out in a place that my thirst will not profit from."

"What does that mean?" A blond-haired man asked but didn't care for an answer. I kind of have blond hair also, some brown, actually, mostly brown.

"That means, that means control man." I had this bad habit of pretending to know what to say. "Watch?" I took the beer from his loose grasp and poured it on the sidewalk. "That is control, you not caring about a drop of booze that is wasted."

"Yeah, but I care about the money I spent on it!"

"Don't worry about money, here take this." I reached into my pockets and had already forgotten again that they were empty. "Ah, it seems I have forgotten my wallet, but don't worry friend, I will pay you ten times what you have lost, just as long as you promise to remember the lesson I have taught you today."

He looked at me as if there was never supposed to be a bad moment in his life, though glad to have an excuse to walk away. But I did exactly as my brain told me just to spite God and his plan. "You have ordered me to suffer, yet I only get happier every second! Your own creation laughing at you! What do you say now?" No one directly answered my prayer, God or the bar guests that were hurrying back inside. The only real justice would be for God to place upon me the fate of meeting a beautiful woman, falling in love, getting married, having kids, buying a house, and then make me fearful of loss and glue me to anticipations of gold watches and tee times. Man, that would be a laugh back in my face.

It was time to get back in my own walls and get drunk by myself. There was a box of Burgundy waiting for me, and besides, The Abbey's patio had emptied out for some weird reason. It was still so early. I wanted to read them Willie's poem and get some real criticism. They would have heard all the wrong things and laughed at the three simple lines, convincing themselves that even they could do better. But they couldn't. They would never create beauty, just more fear, more prejudices, more convenience, and more distractions. I said the poem out loud anyway. The nonexistent audience was better than most. I headed home for the second time.

A few blocks from my house, incidentally the same spot where I turned around the first time and where I turned around that morning, my body went into a limping state, meaning all my body parts practically shut down. This had to be some kind of vortex of consequence. I knew that at some point my body should react exactly the same as the jerky rhythms that I had put into it. If anything else could go wrong it would. I would have to wait by the box of wine and see. Once back in my apartment I fell to the floor and tried to let the twitching just run its course. There was a barren view of black dress shoes under my bed. I hadn't worn them since my dad's funeral. The twitching would eventually pass as all those mornings would pass. The shoes would stay, but all else would pass.

I poured a mug of wine and ate the rest of the crackers as I stared at my wall of memories. The ballroom dancing ad was a solid fifteen feet away from my head, but I was still able to get right onto the dance floor with all of those smiling faces. I spun the heads and lights around while the crowd played tambourines and stomped their goddam feet. It seemed every time my life took a nosedive, my thoughts became vivid like a dream right before you wake, the body flat and useless, the head a tilt away from being priapic, and the eyelids jousting the blood in the brain. When I'm in this state, it's best if other humans aren't involved. I begin to see right through everything and all I want to do is make them solid again, and there's only one way to do that… tear the structure down completely, so we can start to build again. But that was just the Burgundy talking. Its effects were much greater on a saltine cracker dinner.

I put a Charlie Parker album on my record player. My mom, my poor mother, bought the player for me and I love her for it. But every time I play it I have to look her in the eyes from hundreds of miles away and tell her about the real me, the one who could never pretend to be normal. It killed me, but who could lie to the woman who held my hand and led me out of the orphanage. You lie to her and God would really make you happy. Oh, God again! I couldn't get him off my mind, mainly because it seemed he was winning. He was winning because I was sitting on the floor, half on the wood part and half on the rug, sobbing my eyes out. But on the bright side, I was drinking this glorious wine out of a very special coffee mug. Both gifts mind you, just so you don't think that I am a man without support. My friend Luke dropped the wine off one night, along with an acoustic guitar. He said that he only drank good wine and that he was thinking of taking up the bagpipe. That's the kind of friend Luke is. He'd never make you feel guilty about taking something from him.

The coffee cup came from Alex. We were in an old hole in the wall diner in San Francisco having a hung-over breakfast. The Chinese people who ran it kept about a hundred novelty mugs up on the wall, and I don't know if it was because of the 36 hour drinking binge I had been on or what, but my sight zoomed in on one particular mug that read: POOP IS THE SHIT! I said it to myself inside and out. "Yes! Poop is the shit!" At the time it was a moment of clarity, so Alex went to pay the bill and talked the owner into selling it. That's the kind of friend Alex is, the kind that won't let you forget moments of clarity. It's practically the only thing he believes in.

So after the record began making that scratchy hissing sound that told me the moment had passed, it seemed appropriate to call Alex. Now he was living up in New York City, in Brooklyn of all places. We had very awkward phone conversations, so it was just as well that the phone didn't work. Alex and I are true believers in cosmic waves of communication, so I mentally dialed his number and left a cosmic message. "Hey Alex, I'm drunk, but listen to what I have to say. All right, here it is... Everything is valid man... Get it? Everything, truth, lies, phonies, preachers, teachers, the air, the moon, the blood in our veins, you, you, man are valid. I know that God is torturing me, but I also know that it is valid, because above all, above everything else, sadness is valid, happiness is valid, life man, life is valid. This shit isn't for no reason. He is pulling here and pushing there, and when I enter his field of vision he takes a nap. Do you dig it man? I'm a part of God's dreams. He is the most valid… I have to go, I need to write this down." Alex wasn't out there at the moment. He was probably drunk and finishing another novel. That's all he did was vomit out one book after another. I don't think he even starts them, just finishes them. I loved him for it. If we all could excrete with such Immaculate Conception!

That hissing from my blessed record player kept repeating over and over. I couldn't believe how insanely drunk I was after just eight songs. I reached for my notebook on the desk. It fell down and crashed to the floor. A little yellow sticky note lined the inside of the cover. CLUB PLUTO, ABDIEL It was from Luke. This note had hid in my mind, behind the little boy in me who still pirouetted, who still wanted to just play without consequence. I was supposed to go see this Abdiel character about a job. My face lit up and I cosmically screamed, "See Alex, everything is valid!" I hung the note up on the wall beside the Calypso's, and decided to get really drunk, celebratory drunk.

I had a half a bottle of Scotch left over from the last woman to grace these walls, but we won't talk about her, she left behind the whiskey and I'm grateful for that much. My hand nervously adjusted to the pen as if I actually wrote something decent I would vanish into a cloud of steam. My brain thought about the bottle lying on the floor with me. I crawled over to the box of wine again. It seemed to be less needy. I wrote out the beginning sentence of the happiness essay, but only got as far as the introduction. It was a nonsensical account of a funeral by a luminously blue river. Then my mind went back to the bottle. It was calling me like a Siren. There was only one thing to do. I took the blasted bottle, turned it up and into my mouth for as long as I could hold my breath. Then I smashed it against a painting that the same woman gave me. The shattered glass pieces twinkled over my orange couch. The way they shone over the darkness brought a smile to my face. It was all a matter of time before the pieces came back together.

I remember the second before passing out, everything from the first inclination of a dry tacky mouth, then the loss of senses, then the buckle of the knees, the carousel of porcelain ponies jumping up and down on the moon, and my little living room swirling into a tornado. And then seconds, possibly hours later I awoke and my eyes saw nothing but my mural to the most important things to me in the world. There was a picture of Alex and my little sis who was at her first concert. Shit, was it her first concert? I don't know? I couldn't focus. My mind could never focus for more than ten minutes, so that's how I embraced the breaths given to me, like hitting the snooze button on an alarm clock. During this period, one is able to go into the first lucid stage of sleep, but can never reach the comfort of the deep dream stage. Everything else should be lost. Was that the price of happiness? The time lost? Where was my notebook? No, that wasn't it. No... The price of happiness was indubitably... I found my notebook and pen right beside me on the floor. My tools were ready! Before losing all muscular ability, I was able to write down: MY PRICE OF HAPPINESS = SEVENTY-EIGHT CENTS.

one of the best humans I ever met, who incidentally I hardly knew at all...

Day 12,300

When my morning came, it was still dark. I tried to go back to sleep, but sometimes when I was completely still I could feel the world rotating, and that made it hard to sleep, but easy to dream. There were a million chaotic sparks crashing in my head as if it held a bumper-car arena. It was a new day, promising to change my life, a day where I could just show up at a door, shake a hand or two, and have a career of usefulness. Also, I looked forward to getting back out to the woods and making up for all the lost hours. At the very bottom of all my ambition was the hatred of lost time.

I heard my neighbor's alarm clock, which incidentally was the second of the two things that put me back into life. It was either the mail lady at noon, the neighbor's alarm at six in the morning, or it was possible I just wouldn't get up. By the time he had hit snooze four times, the sun had peaked over the horizon and my curtains were glowing with the night's leftover dust.

I went out to check on my tomato plants. They had to be the only thing in the world that made me want to swing in a hammock and whistle. Floyd, my landlord and employer, also happened to be my neighbor in that duplex on the corner of Pine and Bunker Streets. He stood out in the front yard smoking the first of eighty cigarettes that day. He and his wife lived in the much larger side of our duplex, and our bedrooms were only separated by a thin layer of sheet rock and pressed wood.

"Floyd, can I tell you something? That is, be frank this early in the morning?" I rarely waited for people to answer my questions. It would have broken my thought process, and besides, he was really enjoying his first cigarette. "There is something beautiful about the way you hit snooze four times every morning before deciding that it's time to do it again."

"Do what again?"

"Wake up, breathe, start this wonderful life... again."

He scowled at me while using the capacity of his lungs to take a drag.

"I mean, aren't there any times when you're on that third snooze, and you just say, fuck it, I'm getting up. Or even, say you are fully awake on the first snooze, and you say, hey, I hate morning talk shows, let's get out of bed and go fucking do this. Does that ever happen?" I had a habit of squinting with extreme interest whenever I wasn't feigning concern about the answer. "Hm? Does it?"

Floyd, who by the way, was a stand-up kind of guy, one of the best humans I've ever met, who incidentally I hardly knew at all, but with whom I am able to get in quality minutes like this in the mornings. What was I saying? He then proceeded to play dumb, acting as if the fourth alarm was the first, and vice versa and all. Then he accused me of some kind of eavesdropping, questioning my efforts to try and hear as opposed to his efforts to naturally be loud.

"I'm not offended by your misled claims because truthfully the alarm doesn't bother me a bit, and I seriously have never heard one clear word of conversation!" Which isn't totally true because there had been a few nights in which the louder arguments had permeated through as if the walls were screens. One time they were talking about the meaning of life and it was the most evil discussion ever, as if the only thing separating Heaven and Hell was the thin wall between their bedrooms. Floyd's wife, who thinks it's funny to be called *Floyd's wife*, argued that, "You just have to let go of everything and let the waves take you where they will."

Floyd responded, "But that means you'll just drown if you let the waves take you where they will." She told him that was the point, and he called her a "half-tard." Floyd also added that the meaning was easy, we were just supposed to "love one another." I swear my stomach rolled over after hearing that, and it was all I could do not to burn our duplex down right then and there. I went to turn on the gas stove and throw a burning match on my bed, but my gas had been cut off months before and I lost interest before finding a pack of matches.

Floyd apologized after believing my embellishments. I gave him an abrupt farewell before he could ask me about my progress in the woods. It was much too early to speak of work, but snooze alarms and "loving one another" was right up my alley for the agitated rooster. Our backyard was a small fenced-in piece of paradise that I took care of. It was only the size of seven, maybe eight Buicks, and the fence was one of those flat tall wooden blockades. I had it pretty good, better than most if you were to ask me. My tomato plants were about a week or so away from being my breakfast, lunch, and dinner. That is, at least until something better came along. Those days had been cloudy with no anticipation of change. There had been a few times where I had seen God laughing at me in the form of cigarette smoke, and college girls in skirts, and lines to

ATMs. There was a carrot dangling in front of me. There was a donkey in the mirror.

I felt over the greenish-red skin of the tomatoes. Boy that made me feel good, no fucking kidding. I was ready to create that day, looking forward to the night, so I could reflect on all the amazing things that were about to destroy me. My list went in the strict order of: work on happiness essay, go out to the Sisyphus Project for a few hours, get the bar job, and then take my last twenty dollars to get some food and beer. What a day to look forward to! I sat in the grass beside the tomato garden and meditated, concentrating on how beautiful life could be.

I woke up with dirt on the side of my face. The slam of my mailbox took me from my overextended meditation. It was a good nap. My pad and pen waited patiently beside me like old friends that didn't understand what happened to the boy they used to know. I grunted at them and went inside to shower. The Sisyphus Project would have to wait until the next day. I needed to get a job that paid money for Christ's sake. Man can't live by happiness alone! I grabbed my tools and wrote that line down. MAN CAN'T LIVE BY HAPPINESS ALONE. Maybe that could be the title for chapter three or five? One of the odd chapters.

When I was all fixed up, face shaved clean, hair not completely groomed but managed, and my good socks on,

I finished off the box of Burgundy. I was convinced of two things at that moment, that Nietzsche didn't have a sister, and that I needed to be a little drunk in order to not fuck up this job interview. Charlie sat in the driveway waiting for me to give in, but nothing interesting happens when you're driving unless there is wreckage involved. I patted her on the hood and walked on. At the bus stop there was an older man holding the classified section of the newspaper like he had been doing for months.

He came up to me, apologetic and a little annoyed. "Now, last time you said that you were done with us people, that we were all ignorant sheep just following the bus route or some kind of mess like that!"

That didn't sound anything like me, and I became extremely offended. "Whoa! Hold on sir. I'm not sure who you are, or what you are referring to, but I'm just on my way to get a milkshake. Now, if you'll please pardon me."

"What!" The man in disbelief shouted and danced backwards. "Don't even try that shit!"

"Sir, I am sure that we have never met. I'm a genius when it comes to remembering faces. Once upon a time my mother used me as a reference book to who was who at all of her shindigs, galas, and such. You see she was a Broadway star. You may have heard of her, Farla Lapel?" That name was brilliant. It sounded just like someone who you couldn't quite picture. The man's suspicious expression became lighter and he even began to nod as if he believed me. But he wasn't quite convinced, so I had to go on. "Yes, we moved from New York when I was only fourteen and we came here to the South where mother only did the occasional cameo in the town workshop. But boy, in her heyday she could blow away the most unpleasant theater snobs. I even blame myself for our move from the city, for I was a problem child. It seemed the only thing I was good at was remembering faces." I was glowing inside with deceit.

"Yes, yes, Farla Lapel. I believe my daughter is an admirer of her."

"There's no doubt she should be." I couldn't believe the nerve of this man, the way he lied right to my face.

"New York City huh? Always wanted to go up there."

"Yes, it does sound right doesn't it?" I answered truthfully.

"How is your mother now?"

My mother! How dare he ask about my mother! "Unfortunately she has passed, God bless her soul."

"Yes, God bless her soul." His head turned to look up the road for the bus.

"I see you have the classifieds there. How's the search?"

"Good, good, something going to pop up any day now." The man said as if he really believed it.

"This might be your lucky day friend. My name is Luke." I gave him another deserving fib. "I have an acquaintance that is looking for a good man to run his bar. Now you look like a good man, look like you've done some bar work before, what do you think?" I said like JP Oglethorpe. He agreed with me; like a sheep he followed along with everything I said. He would be fine as long as he got hired before the real Luke actually set eyes upon him. Luke would kill me for giving away his reference, but it felt good to do something for the nice man who thought I was a maniac. "Just ask for Abdiel. Tell him Luke sent you for the bar job." I told him as the bus was pulling up. "Here's the address, just up the road." He took it and ran for the bus while the whole time thanking me like a moron. I pretended to go order a milkshake at Dairy Queen.

"How may I help you?" The counter girl had a silver ring through her lip.

"Just this napkin thanks." I stared at her lip. How absurd. What kind of spell was she under? I thought of asking the girl, but some things you just can't question, especially if the thing is a human. The bus rolled away. I felt like doing a cartwheel or climbing a telephone pole.

What a scenario! "Farla Lapel!" I said to the Dairy princess. She flipped me off. I repeated the scene over in my head, from him accusing me of loving commuters too much, all the way to his desperation to get to a job that was mine. He would never remember me as the bus stop lunatic, but the saint who blessed his life with the possibility of money. One of my best friends, Sign Guy, was working the opposite corner, where the sun wasn't suppressed. He waved at me.

"Did you see that?" I yelled.

He shook his head.

"Farla Lapel!"

He gave me a thumbs-up. "You got a dollar Farla?"

"Not today my friend."

He held up his sign. GUILT CAN RUIN YOUR DAY.

I walked all the way home on my toes, floating above that guilt.

It seemed whenever there was a busted bottle of Scotch decorating my couch and an empty wine box in my trash can, it made me sleepy. I wilted into the fetal position on the floor beside my bed. I was just going to nod off for a few minutes while taking in some music. There was still work to be done. I had gotten behind eight or maybe twelve hours, and even though I could get it over in one long day, it seemed better to just catch up an extra hour at a time. Above my bed on the adjoining wall of Floyd's bedroom was a map of the globe. It helped me dream of palm trees and paper mountains. They were both much easier to burn than climb. My mind bonded with the map and I became fixated on all the people in the world sitting around and wondering about life, in that tiny little space. Man that made me nuts. Then after a few minutes of nodding off, going in and out of a nightmare of a shag carpet strangling me, I realized that I had given my job away. Once again, moral complexities would keep me from eating. Why didn't I just give Sign Guy a dollar? What was wrong with me? It was as if I couldn't control anything rational. That had to be at the top of the blunder list, at least for the month.

My want for money was building up. Mind you, I didn't need it. There must have been $200 worth of books and music sitting up there on my shelf just waiting to be put back into the world. The shelf held all the world's solutions. I opened up *Stranger in a Strange Land* and pulled out my last twenty-dollar bill. The pages could finally rest. All I needed was a newspaper and a bit of food. Then by the next day there would be a big shit-eating-grin moron who would have me as their employee, ready to make me civil and complacent. I couldn't wait.

As I passed by the newspaper machines, my fingers made sure the right crinkle of currency was still in my pocket. I won't even get into how much money I've lost just on the pure basis of looking at the wrong machine or lighting the wrong candle. This particular orange machine needed thirty-five cents to provide me with opportunity. I went inside the grocery store to buy some cheap noodles and make change. Apparently the store was dying. There were these fluorescent hospital lights all over the ceiling. It sure as hell put people in a different light. There was a point in which my head felt as if it was forming blisters. I became disoriented and lost. Aisle number eight, cereals and crackers. Aisle number eleven, frozen breakfast foods. Aisle number one, fruits and vegetables. My eyes looked down and woke up. It seems I was stalking a woman that couldn't put a strawberry in her cart without it tipping over. Maybe that's why I was following her, the vision of having all that food crash to the white tile floor made me giggle with delight. She finally went to the checkout line. There was the sound of receipts printing, scanners bleeping, shopping carts squeaking, hospital lights buzzing, bags being filled, and automatic doors opening and shutting. It was like living vicariously through a lion that trudged through the jungle with blood on its lips and a dead elk hanging over its neck.

I ended up in the last aisle with the coolers. The reduction in heat helped me think much clearer. This one brand of beer exclaimed on its label that each beer was only 85 calories. It got me thinking about how many calories regular beer had, because the noodles were only 200 per box. If I could drink one beer and get almost the same amount of calories and maybe even more nutrition, then why wouldn't I buy beer? My mind raced with some kind of false aggravated excitement. I studied each brand to calculate the cost to calorie ratio. Finally, I found the case that would suit my needs the best, that is, that would feed me for the next few days.

Before finishing my shopping, another overloaded cart caught my eye. I pretended to feel avocados while she was topping off her hunt with a tub of sour cream. She was much more focused than I was, but equally as fascinated. I named her Ava after the goddess of squeezable fruit. I saw her as someone that could save me, the way she picked her items so patiently, almost empathetically. That's how she would be with me, that's how she would take care of me. She's most likely was this way because she has some major flaw like a prosthetic leg or a speech impediment. That's how people become patient, flaws or seclusion. I would love her despite whatever is fucked up with her and she would be patient with me, and I would love her unconditionally.

She looked up at me once, and it obviously flustered her. She began to move faster. I kept following her, not even trying to hide it. I made bets with myself on how many kids she had. Only two? "No, definitely three." She got in line and I hurried back over to the coolers and grabbed my case of beer. There were only two lines open, the regular and the express. I feigned a lackadaisical confusion, and settled in behind Ava in the non-express line. She turned and gave my one item a look as if it was a hamster cage. But I stayed strong, analyzing each and every item that Ava was taking home to her family. Man, that must feel great to have the satisfaction of nurture and survival and love all wrapped up in paper Shop Easy bags. I imagined her pulling up in her 4-wheel drive SUV, feeling so good about bringing home everyone's favorite foods, honking the horn to get them all out of their rooms, feigning humility when the dog goes nuts over the doggy treats, having her husband come out to help bring in the slaughter, and then as they all help put it away in the cabinets, they tell about what they did that day. Fuck, that must be something weird. Anyway, by the time the beer was rung up I had an idea for the happiness essay. The main character would be a stalker that follows people who abide the automated crosswalks. The stalker would be fascinated with the obedience of lights. I would name it *The Moron Factory.* By the time this idea had truly conformed and I had whistled out a few lines, I was almost home without food or a newspaper. But it didn't matter. All that mattered was writing the essay. With a case of beer, a pen and paper, I could occupy dozens of ten-minute lives. Who could ask for more than that?

The first swallow of beer hit my stomach like an old friend saying hi with a hug. The thing with alcohol was I could stop at any time and just laugh at sobriety. What I was doing was strictly dietary and even a bit phony-artsy, but dying that night was as good as dying twenty years from then, or even better actually. The ten-minute lives went by along with the beers and before I realized it, I had strayed from my goal. So in protest, I sat down on the carpet and began to turn out words with no regard for structure or theme.

By the sixth beer I had written out seventeen pages and I began to sob with happiness. I thanked God that he didn't let me go to that job. I was so blessed. That bar would have eaten my soul alive. Who in their right mind would ever pay $15 for a glass of fermented grapes? They couldn't even take two seconds of their lives to realize that nothing matters, and everything coexists together with or without them. Yes, the gentleman from the bus stop would be better suited for the job. He probably had a family to feed, a mortgage wrapped around his neck, bills to pay, a sense of satisfaction to pay, and all the other things you have to do in order to live. Yes, he'll fit in just perfect there.

All I had to do was just take some of my finest books down to good old Hans at the bookshop. Hans had never let me down when needing a little inspiration in the form of literature or money. That first edition of *The Rosy Crucifixion* was probably a thousand dollar roll of toilet paper. Hans would let loose an orgasm that he had saved since coming to America if the trilogy was placed on his counter. But I would start low, start with the other stuff, paperbacks from Anderson and Celine and such. There was no sense in harping on the future. It only existed in the inadequacy of the present. At that moment I had some celebrating to do, some festivity for the amazing seconds orbiting my head, some hand clapping for the possibility of choices, hand clapping for bellies filled with juice, turkey, semen, laughs, and pills, pills from all charges of brain waves, duplicating masturbation, stamina, comfort, drowsiness, and oranges.

By the time the eleventh beer can was folding in my hand, I figured to be up to almost 2000 calories. Boy, I was full! I looked inside the fridge and that half-stick of butter and bottle of Korbel XP champagne advised me to take a break. Sometimes one has to listen to inanimate objects without speculation. I pretended to ice skate over to my CD collection. There were albums there that would turn a music store clerk on for at least three hundred snoozes. I eyed the titles while down on one knee like Rodin's The Thinker sculpture. I chose the most obscure of the lot as an inside joke, laughing to myself until even I didn't get it. I eventually got together ten popular discs that only an idiot would turn away. I then put on my sandals, got a beer, and headed out with my sacrificial music. There was a used CD store only about a mile and a half away. I was sure that it was open until midnight.

The clock in The CD Depot read 10:38. I put the ten cases up on the elevated counter. The clerk, sad-eyed and stoned, or maybe just lazy-eyed and stoned was about a foot above me like he was on stage. "We stop buying at 10:00." He pointed to some sign on the door that I didn't look at.

"Who's this playing?" I asked. It sounded like some droning English rock band.

"This?" He pointed to the ceiling. It was the only music playing.

"Uh huh, this." Even I wasn't that drunk.

"Why?"

"Because they're pretty good." I lied.

The clerk looked at my ten discs and said, "Yeah, they're pretty decent, but I don't know who they are. Once you know who it is then the spiritual aspect is ruined."

I wanted to tell him that I was just writing about the lack of spirituality, but instead I replied, "That's true." I was unsure if I believed it or not. "But what if I wanted to purchase it?"

"Oh, it's The New Pornographers, middle aisle, third of the way down on the left."

"Seriously?" He had me.

"No man, I just talked to you about spirituality."

"That's true." I looked behind me. There was no one there. "So can I have about thirty dollars for these CDs? I'm not looking to make a killing off them, just a reasonable price, you know?" I looked behind me again.

"I told you this also. We stop buying at 10:00." He pointed to the sign again and then to the clock behind him. "And it is 10:45 right now."

"Do you buy CDs?"

"Yes, I do."

"So what's the difference?"

"The difference is, the later you stay open, the better chance you have of getting robbed. So if I show someone that I just gave a hundred dollars to a seller then they know that I'm keeping that kind of dough behind the counter, but as it is, I only keep change for a twenty!" He sounded upset.

"How about theoretically... theoretically?"

"Um, let's see." He looked over the titles. "Um, yes, nothing."

"How-"

He shushed me with his pointer, "Favorite part!" He began to shake like he was possessed. He felt the music and let it take him over. I closed my eyes and tried to bond with the waves. The droning had progressed to a harmonic orchestral rock. It took a small period of seconds, but when it hit me, my shoulders and feet took over. I'm sure it was a horrible scene, one fat post-grungy clerk and one lump of robotic flesh pushing the limits of rhythm. The song ended and we stopped dancing. "Alright, here's my final offer. Keep them behind the counter, with my name on top of the stack, and tomorrow morning I'll come first thing and we'll take care of it then." I said and he laughed sincerely as if I was telling him a joke. Then when he realized that I was just a serious anthropological experiment, he shook his head fearfully. "We're going to close in a few minutes, so just bring them back tomorrow."

I wanted to tell him that I had walked over an hour to get there and I didn't want to walk all the way back with the stupid CDs, but instead, "Just keep'em man." And I walked out of the stupid goddamn jingling door. My mind was glowing. What luck! It was as if my guardian angel got drunk and passed out, only to wake up just enough to laugh at the hysterics. Then it occurred to me that just asking for a bag would have been another logical option. I went back. The door was locked. It was dark inside the store, but I could tell someone was in there. I knocked, but no one came. And that's when I really began to understand my purpose for the night. It wasn't anything I ever expected, but then again it never was.

The Abbey sat right in my path toward home. There were two bartenders working, one that didn't know me and one that knew me all too well. I used to try and convince him of our connection because we were the same height when I sat down, but he would just humor me to a point. He gave me the old stink-eye as soon as I stepped foot up to the bar. There was a redneck beauty beside my future barstool. He came at me with the conviction of a man tired of dealing with shit. I took the upper hand. "Just water please, I'm not boozing any longer." I put a dollar tip down for the water. He served me quickly. What a moron. He would be a perfect example for my happiness essay.

I glanced around waiting for words to ruin me. The conglomerate of mouths in motion confused me like a cornered animal. I was uncomfortable, nervous about what might happen, where God might take me in this scenario. My mind flipped, turned, searched for escape. The good lord gave me no choice but to write poems.

The brunette beside me put her hand on my arm and asked, "John, can you-" She turned to see it was the wrong man. "Oh, sorry. I thought you were someone else."

"I am someone else, I've always been someone else. Have you ever been someone else?" I asked her. She had on maroon lipstick and smelled nice, like a million other actresses, but nice.

"What?" She was either intrigued or hard of hearing.

Before answering I noticed a jagged scar hidden underneath the makeup on her cheek. "I'll never be John. Will you ever not be you?"

"You know John?"

"I know all Johns."

"What do you mean, will I ever not be me?" She took a sip from some pink concoction. Something that she was supposed to drink.

"Have I made you ask that question for the first time in your life?"

"What the fuck are you talking about?"

"Now see, you've probably asked *that* question a million times. What the fuck I'm talking about is beauty, real beauty, not the kind that people see in you from across the room. The kind I can see close-up right now." I chugged my glass of water, almost nervous over continuing with my act.

She thought for a whole two seconds. "I don't know? I don't know what you're talking about." She refused to acknowledge the truths inside of her, the truths of tragedy. I couldn't stop staring at her scar.

"I'm talking about tragedy. You've affected me. You've affected every person in here that was intimidated by your beauty." She didn't know how to respond to what seemed like compliments, so I took it further than any of us expected. "Can I touch it? Let me touch it and make it real."

"Excuse me!" She was shocked. I wasn't sure why. Did she think the scar was hidden under her mask? "You fucking pervert!" She made sure that everyone around heard her. The men she was with turned around, confused, and generally stupid, but very keen to this common Southern distress call. It was time for them to play their roles as men. I sat there calmly, waiting to see what unfolded. You see, I wasn't a troublemaker, just a dismissive observer. The manly men tried to find out what was going on. I finished my water while looking on just like the rest, like I was unsure of what was going on also.

"You!" My old bartender buddy called me out.

"Hey, what's up buddy?" I thought he finally wanted to be friends.

"I knew you'd start your shit!"

"I don't know what you mean. The young lady apparently didn't know that most beautiful part on her is the scar on her face."

"This guy?" One of the manly men pointed at me. He had this cologne on that reminded of the pink soap in gas station bathrooms. It was nice. Things were starting to get exciting. I jokingly pointed at myself because he expected a much more mystified man. After that there were many voices and they all seemed to be yelling in my direction. I was the most popular person at the party. The girl and her two protectors discussed it more, as in a war negotiation scene. The barkeep gave the signal to my big friend at the door.

"So that's it?" I asked him.

He looked me dead in the eyes, secured by the two feet of wood in between us. "Yeah, and that's the last time, don't come back." They had told me this before.

The giant bouncer approached the bar, unsure of whom he was coming for because it seemed I was the calmest person there. "This one." My bartender friend pointed at me. Of course the two cowards became brave when the security showed up. Gas station bathroom soap took a swipe at me, but he didn't really want to feel flesh collapsing into his fist. He did graze my ear. Then the bouncer locked onto me, and took my undefended body toward the door. It's weird. No one actually ever asked me to leave. Things could have been easier for everyone if they just thought for two seconds, but it seemed to be the pattern that fit me. The scarred beauty had this satisfied smirk as the bouncer glided my two hundred pounds across the floor.

"They can see! They can see your tragedy!" I screamed at her.

All eyes were glued to the scene. The music stopped and the stage was moving outside. I became happy that everyone blinked out of their sleep as if the sun had just come up. As the stares grew, my urge to give them more tripe grew. The bartender followed us outside. I easily broke free from the brute's arms and bluffed at the bartender. He jumped backwards. I just wanted to keep the show going, not hurt anyone except myself. Pain was the only thing I could trust to be real. The bouncer caught me quickly and then stepped it up a notch with his grip. That time it was more of a chokehold with a stumbling drag.

The brunette was in my path of sight. Her expression had softened as if she was just starting to understand what was happening. I think I was in love with her.

The cool midnight air caught my attention before I could really focus on the situation at hand. My mind drifted with thoughts of September and all the amazing possibilities of autumn. Then he dropped me to the sidewalk. Many of the rubbernecks had followed my backwards feet outside. I felt like the doomed bull in a Peruvian Coliseum. It was as if everyone in the world was against me. All they saw was a man who didn't care, but that wasn't true, it was the opposite, I cared way too much, I cared beyond the needs of anyone.

"Have a good night sir." The bouncer said sincerely, and that made me angrier than anything. How dare he act like I deserved respect! Out of all these lying fuckers who came out to see me get beaten, I at least expected one person to be honest with me. Throw me to the ground, stomp on me, call me the scum of the Earth, but do not pretend that I should have a good night, and do not call me sir! Scar-face said something to her man friend and laughed. I was willing to let them all win up until those last two things. I would have taken a beating for their pleasure and guilt all night if that's what they wanted. But at that moment I selfishly wanted to win. "Is that all you have nigger?" I said, still on the ground.

The bouncer stopped walking away, and all the smiling faces turned to a mixed up terror. It was quite hilarious to see the white crowd become scared of a word that they didn't say at that moment, but had obviously used it in private before.

The bouncer came back at me and asked as his duty, "What did you say?"

He knew what I said, and I didn't have to repeat it. Him asking was just another clue of fear and rationalism. He could only fathom that an insane person would ever say such a thing to a giant person like him. But ultimately he used his fear against me when I told him what I said. I stood up, face wide, and I think I may have even closed my eyes before feeling my nose get crushed and the sound of humans in shock and disgust. The next thing I remember was being helped up to my feet. It was the bouncer. Who knows how long it had been? The crowd was gone as far as I could see. My eyelids were practically swollen shut.

"You're one messed up motherfucker." He told me.

"That word has been used a lot tonight... motherfucker, that is, not nigger."

"Yeah, well, I guess you got what you wanted." He almost chuckled.

"Wanted? No, I got what I needed. We all have to find our own way to survive. Mine appears to be different."

"Shut up man!" The short bartender said. He and one other guy were smoking a cigarette in the distance. "See what you get fucker. You deserved that for a long time."

"Deserve what? I just have a fucked up face." I walked sideways trying to catch my balance. The bouncer laughed while shaking his head. He realized his punch was useless for his purpose, and just a prop for my own. There were too many people in the world that aren't willing to get cracked in the face. Mediocrity is the enemy of creation.

"Now is the time." I told the bouncer. "Now is the time to tell me to have a good night, now is the time to call me sir. The order was off. The order seems to always be off."

He nodded. I left these half completed statues, proud of myself, relishing the tingle inside my cheeks.

I cut through the parking lot on my way home. The brunette with the scar was leaning against the front of a car while her friend, probably John, was puking onto the cracked blacktop. She eyed me for a few seconds and then asked from about thirty feet away, "What's wrong with you? Why did you do that?"

I didn't have to think about the answer. "I never had a choice not to do it." God has a plan that no one can understand or question, and so did I.

Orion looked down on me, judging each lazy step,
finding ways to conspire with the devil...

Day 12,301

I woke up the next morning with an astounding headache. My face felt like a helium balloon held down by a cinder block. My bewildered and smiling expression stretched out the pain. I couldn't believe my luck. What a night! I couldn't wait to fuck up again. It couldn't happen fast enough in my mind. My fists pounded against the mattress. All those people out in the world trying to get it perfect, trying to walk the tightrope into paradise. Oh God! Why would you make someone so delusional and hypocritical? All I wanted to do was die lightly, that is with fewer boxes, with less skin cells. Dust was the enemy of living.

Everyone always talks about how they don't want to die alone. I like the idea of being alone in my last days. It seems awful to have someone by your bedside, feeling sorry for you, or wishing they could go home, or wondering what the football score is, or wondering what they will inherit once you don't exist anymore.

My decision was to stay in bed that day. It would be much cheaper that way and no one would be offended. Maybe I would just drift off on a burning rowboat and let everyone else be free of my thoughts. Finally, a rational thought! But, my legs didn't follow the vision of my heart. I went out to the backyard, stepping into the shadows below my feet. I always envisioned my shadows as something that I would meet on the other side of the world, never something I would step into in my own backyard. They were like poop.

My tomato plants were exactly as I had hoped, almost ready. If everything in life just remained almost ready! A big pile of anticipation stacking up into a tower. Then death could be the time in which one could pick and choose the fulfillments. One could only dream.

All of these thoughts of anticipation made me pick off the biggest of the tomatoes. I began squeezing it and after it was ruined, and after the juice ran down my fingers, wrist, and forearm, I understood why my face was so black and blue. I licked the sour red liquid off my hand, grasping at any nutrition available. Life flowing over my arm, life flowing inside my arm, inspiration to open one's eyes and live! I then went back to bed, closing the blinds in the kitchen before closing my eyes.

My imaginary alarm clock kept forcing my balloon head to rise. It was difficult to grasp the time. It was dark out and I still had the same clothes on, so I thought it would be nice to take a walk. At least in the night shadows, no one could see my busted nose. Floyd's clock read 11:39. Maybe I would offer to wash his windows later. There was a light film of dirt that made the glass tricky to see through. Anyway, it was almost midnight, and I was happy that I woke up before the day had passed.

The neighborhood was always quiet, but that night it was as if they had all finally went through with their cult suicide pact. I took my usual path to escape, but this time my purpose was to walk the train tracks. The day that danced just a few minutes in front of me was my father's anniversary of death. He was an old railroad man before going into the ministry. The railroad kept him away from home, and the ministry kept him away from life. Then about a decade ago he got away from both of these by ending his time on this world. I took my first step on the tracks, looked east and saw eternity, then looked west and saw the same, but north and south were just safety nets under the high-wire. My vision went west. There was an old train depot where dozens of the tracks joined together and then separated into the vast universe of America. I loved to just sit right in the middle of the cluster and feel the ghosts pass through me. There hadn't been a train to roll through there in at least ten years. I got this information secondhand from this hobo I met about three summers ago. When he told me this pertinent fact, he said it in a manner as if he blamed my generation, as if we invented convenience for convenience sake. We were specifically intelligent in prevalent cases of making life more comfortable, but for God's sake, it was never on purpose. If any of this carried intention, then we would all learn to stop breathing at conception.

After an hour or so I got to the hub of the old town. I draped my body over the gravel and railroad ties. There were several constellations at this view. I couldn't quite understand the content feeling that overcame me there. Life becomes very weird whenever you kind of wish you died that night and at the same time you pray to feel the exact same way the next night. Orion looked down on me, judging each lazy step, finding ways to conspire with the devil, laughing at every falter, yet still on its way to being destroyed by daylight. I yelled something in gibberish to the hunter, "Artemis over mountain, love of goats!" Humans don't have to make sense to Gods, because we invented them. I got off the ground and went inside the abandoned depot. There was a broken clock, but I'm pretty sure the time was correct. It was up on a wall above what appeared to be the main check-in desk. I went behind it and waited with an intense eagerness for something to happen. Nothing did. I banged on the rotten wood, "Goddamn it!" It was so hard to be a failure. I had tried to be a success, but it made me miserable. Sometimes when I ate cake and ice cream, a vision came to me, a vision of forgetting about the air, and it always made me happy. Once, just the last time I had to wear my coat, my mom asked me, "Why are you so happy?" I was watching football, sitting on my childhood couch, and eating her famous coconut cake with a side of chocolate ice cream. I looked up at her, maybe even smiled, and said, "Well, I can understand why I'm happy, but I can't understand why you think I'm happy." She did her classic hand flip with eye roll, and then walked away.

    I thought about my sister. It was way too early to call her, but if I passed near a pay phone she would have to be woken up. There was something very important I needed to tell her. She was sixteen and as far as I know that's a good age to start learning about tragedy. It was nice to have a daily goal, something to keep the mind occupied.

    Before I go any further, you should know something very important. Ester and I are siblings by contract, not blood. Her blood parents adopted me at the age of seven, which was nine years before she was born. My biological parents apparently had mental issues or something. That's all.

It's funny how I can't remember what day it is or the last time I ate a real meal, but I can remember my days in the orphanage as if I were watching it on a video. I blame the clarity on extreme hope and overwhelming American dreams. Mr. Beverly taught me how to read as I learned how to talk, and by the age of seven I was reading everything from Twain to Dickens. Granted I didn't understand the authors, but I understood what I wanted out of the story. I understood that I was going to escape that awful place and make something of myself. I was going to have adventures and success.

The day that I was adopted was a disappointing moment in which it felt like someone other than myself saved me. But what do you do? I wanted to be Tom Sawyer, but settled to be Heathcliff. I had no real friends in the orphanage, just books and imaginary heroes. They told me the truth. The kids there didn't know they were in competition. The cutest puppies would always win. But what is winning? Living in comfort? Just like most things in life, the simple daily activities become what can be defined as comfort. Sleeping in a large room with dozens of other unwanted kids, eating in a large room with dozens of other hungry mouths, and bathing in a large room with dozens of other dirty bodies became the comfort of what we knew. Whether it happens inside the walls of an orphanage or inside the walls of the thousands of little houses surrounding me now. I haven't stopped trying to escape.

Now almost a quarter of a century later my heroes have changed to old drunk poets, homeless train hoppers, and tragically recluse tap dancers.

Before leaving the tracks and going north, I envisioned an old boxcar train howling through the night with me huddled in the shadows of its corners. My eyes followed the stars home, avoiding the moon. Failures can see the moon looking down on all the people with purpose. The vision of a new day made me throw up in my yard. Only a few spurts of dirty saliva came up. I hurried inside and made it to bed before the sun showed its claws. I didn't have the stomach for it. The spotted sheet felt good over my head, safe enough, and warm enough. I said a prayer for my dad's soul and escaped again.

God and the devil had some weird bet going on...

Day 12,302

I thought about just giving in and going back to teaching. I thought about maybe calling the girl who gave me the painting, go on a proper date, and try not to take for granted that very few people in this world will ever love me the way they love youth, possibility, and potential. Maybe I could start watching the same TV show every week. Maybe I will have kids with this woman and teach them about life and then live vicariously through their beautiful naïve minds. Maybe, maybe, maybe... all those goddamn times waking up, thousands and thousands of mornings, hangovers, cups of coffee, and regrets. But either way I got out of bed unsure which side I would take that day. In the mirror was a beaten man, not only with a crooked smashed nose, but eyes behind blacked-out binoculars. I'm not sure how many more punches I could take, or even better, how many more I needed. My head felt like an infinite number of plates. When one breaks there's always another behind the progression. The saving grace was that the reflection held a beginning and an end, a small timeline that seemed like a whole life when looking from the outside in.

The picture of my sister was still beside the phone. Inside *Zen and the Art of Motorcycle Maintenance* was a phone card that had some minutes left on it. I put it in my pocket and went out to the backyard. Had it already been a full day since I was last out there? It seemed like a week, yet the same steaks of green were over top the devilish flesh like no time had passed at all. One of the tomatoes had an insect nibbling into its black crater. Though very tempted to thump it away, I decided to leave it. I hoped that one day I'd find myself lost on top of a giant tomato with a straw and a pillow. That reminded me that I still hadn't really eaten if you don't count the crackers and all that beer. It seemed I would eventually have to sell some of my books. The idea of all this malnutrition and putting books back on the shelf had my spirits up.

Floyd's wife was on the other side of the fence. She was humming a song that completely annoyed me. Maybe it wasn't the song though, maybe it was the way she hummed it. It seemed that life was very manageable for her, and not in the way of wealth or happiness, but in the way of uselessness. It bothered me that someone could be so arrogant, that someone could just ignore that life was going on right in front of her face, but instead of recognizing it and shouting to the heavens, she fucking hums a song, she fucking waters flowers she doesn't see, and she fucking devours the air without hearing the screams. I became loosely associated with civil behavior and decided to strangle her.

"Hello Floyd's wife, beautiful day." I said.

She couldn't even be bothered to respond. Floyd's wife smiled as if she really meant it.

"Off to the woods." I threw in for some reason. Why did I care if she knew my work schedule? The work would get done no matter what. It's not as if Floyd has ever said anything to me when I've gotten behind. Granted, that time was the furthest the Sisyphus Project had gotten away from me. Floyd's wife looked over her shoulder at me as I walked away. One sweet day I would put my hands around her throat and put her out of her misery. "Alright then." I waved. "Have a wonderful morning."

There was a pay phone up near Dairy Queen. Sign Guy was just setting up. He had a milk crate with a pillow, a real paradise. "Morning. Almost tuxedo weather." I said. He just held up his new sign. INNER HAPPINESS IS DERIVED FROM KINDNESS. He wouldn't make much money that day. For some reason humans don't feel sorry for people who use words like *derived*. They want someone they can relate to, someone that wears tragedy on their sleeve, someone with a limp, a speech impediment, one testicle, a goiter, in short, someone displaying a defect in which choice wasn't granted by the gods. But truth is, none of us ever had a choice, none of us knew what that brilliant ball of light in the sky was until it burned our nose, and we all keep our tragedies in our pockets, and the man who claims different has the defect of delusion.

Sign Guy threw a pebble at my leg. "You alright?"

"Me? Why I'm infectiously happy." I mumbled while walking to the pay phone. It was nice that Sign Guy cared about me so much. He was one of my best friends.

My stomach began to grumble when the smell of burgers and fries wafted by me. I picked up the phone, but just stared out at the cracked plastic tables. There were two blue-collar working men with dirt and paint all over their clothes. They ate like pigs. I loved it. God bless us animals. God bless our lunch hour.

I called Ester.

"Hello." She sounded like she just woke up.

"Hey." I was a horrible phone conversationalist. I preferred to leave messages. "Sorry to wake you, but I've been up awhile and decided that you should talk to me today before nightfall, because we're not even promised that."

"Hmm..." Ester doesn't actually have conversations. She prefers for me to just talk until I'm done, then, well, then nothing, we say goodbye.

"Now listen, I know you're tired and I know that it'd be easy just to pretend to listen to me like everyone else does, but this one time is the time to pay attention. Now, first of all let's just go ahead and get it out of the way. Today is dad's suicide anniversary and I know it shouldn't be called an anniversary, and it's not a happy occasion or anything, but what I have to tell you is about him."

I waited for a response. She may have yawned away from the receiver.

"It's something that took me a long time to understand and get over. It's... it's that 99% of all of us humans are too weak to carry out our burdens, and blaming people for their natural weaknesses only continues the epidemic. Vince Lombardi said, 'Fatigue makes cowards out of humans.' He was using it for football, but it fits any aspect of life. It's why dogs will fight to the death, and we fight until we're bothered. Do you dig it?"

It took her about ten seconds to answer. "Yes."

I believed her, because she could have said yes right away.

"Good, because you're only sixteen, and you haven't become tired yet. Humans get tired and scared and complacent, and they stop driving fast. It's why our insurance is lower, we stop being risks, and start being cowards. I went around a long time blaming and ridiculing anyone who displayed faults in my presence. My high horse was the Trojan horse, so to speak. It was hard for me to realize that humans make decisions from two basic roots. From fear or faith. Our society is kept in check by fear and has been since the first time that one person had to make a decision with another. We know nothing else but to believe in faith, yet not practice it. Now in this case, and I have to tell you that I'll hang up right now if you don't want to hear this, because it's going to be hard, so do you want me to hang up or go on?"

Again, a long silence. "I don't know."

"I know you don't know, but do you want to hear the truth or not?"

"Yes." She said softly, and I know her well enough to know that that meant to go on.

"Okay, well, dad being a preacher had many more burdens than most, he had a whole congregation of burdens, he had many fears to deal with, and to expect a simple country preacher in this new globalized planet to carry out these things is ridiculous. As an outsider, I suppose it would be ideal to teach faith and just hope it sinks in and works in most of your immediate church members and whatever little world we lived in. When you're alone you reap no repercussions, only the individual is to blame for his own actions and decisions. You could even say that these people are in fear of fear. But dad wasn't alone, he was never alone, even when sitting in his church on a Tuesday afternoon. He was like a wet sponge that would never dry. He was surrounded by fear and the power of God, and even the ego to know that he was a messenger kept him mentally intact all the way up until the end." A giant belch distracted me. It was one of the contract workers. They were finishing up their trough session. They made me sick. "I learned so much from dad, but when he died, I made a conscious decision to forget everything he taught me. I needed to leave my friends and family and just be a man without the responsibility of letting my loved ones down. That sounds really bad saying it out loud, but what I mean and meant is that I knew from that point of finding dad's body that anyone that tries to do some good in our culture is going to let someone down. But this has nothing to do with anything, except don't be afraid to let people down. I ran, but you don't have to run. Dad killed himself, but there are so many ways to kill one's self without a pill, or a tall building, or a gun. For instance, he killed himself when he stopped working the railroad and became a preacher. Do you get it?" I asked but didn't wait for the obvious answer. "Anyway, to cut to the chase, Christ you haven't even had your orange juice and pop tarts yet. Don't worry, it'll all be over soon, and you'll once again be able to get back to your normal life with mom and whatever boyfriend you're hiding from her. Yeah, um..." I distracted myself because I didn't like the thought of her with boys yet.

"So after learning why actions had to be completed, I began to care deeply about humans as a whole, even though I thoroughly despised them as friends, and entertainers, and distractions. It was a slow progression, but I found the way to carry the world's burdens without putting them on my shoulders. And I know that I've been driving this stuff into your brain since you could hear, and that's what worries me. I don't want to make you into the monster that I am, and it's too late to change you from someone that's going to try to be extraordinary, so I'm using dad as an example and partly me to convey that you have to find a way to realize the soul of truth within you and whatever step you take or whatever watch you live by, make sure the world isn't making decisions for you. Dad let his little world pull him by the words of the bible and the expectations of someone higher than a human. If you want to understand life and make changes you have to find that .0001 percent of your mind that no one in history has ever touched. That's the blockade of evil, the creator of beauty. You following me here lil sis?"

She didn't answer.

"Sis?"

"Yeah." She exhaled heavily.

"Do you understand, because I don't even know what I'm saying?"

"Uh huh."

"Listen, I'm sorry I woke you with my crazy ideas."

She was one smart cookie, but still, she was sixteen and tired.

"Just believe in faith and you'll be fine. That's all I wanted to say. Dad lost faith because he was going by someone else's book. Faith, okay? I'll talk to you later." I got ready to hang up.

"What about just being a regular person and doing what you're supposed to do, living right, living by society's rules, being happy and sad, creating families that go to church and eat dinner together. Is there something wrong with that? It seems like a lot less hassle. Why do we need to progress when we're just going to die anyway?" Ester said out of nowhere. I was a bit taken back. She did this about once a year. Even when she as young as five or six years old she'd shock the hell out of me after being silent for months at a time.

"Well, that's fine if you think that's what's going to work for you, but I'm certain it's too late for you to just decide to be a regular person." I paused to see if she had more to say, but she didn't. "I personally believe that we have some duty to share what our minds have invented. And also, I believe that there can't be many humans that stray from what you were suggesting. It's definitely ideal in some ways to have a million poets and painters skipping down the countryside, but the world just can't work that way at this moment. So there is something to be said for just following the wide path that most of us are shown at an early age. My problem with the concept, is the human not recognizing it, or recognizing anything for that matter. It's fine if you decide to live out the pattern of most, but there's a pattern that goes along with it that makes the person believe that their senses are the only things that exist, what they see is what is, what they feel is what is. They are useless capsules of blood and bones that have no duty except to take up space. And before, these useless bodies would die off because of survival of the fittest, but now humans have progressed into an arrogant period of time when the laziest most useless idiots can survive without lifting a single brain cell of consideration. We are regressing as a whole, and it seems there are less and less people who are trying to shake things up, because of couches and running shoes. Oh God you got me all worked up, I'm sorry. What do you think?"

"I don't know. I kind of think you're a hypocrite I guess."

"Yes!" I was blown away. "I'll always seem that way, maybe because I couldn't fathom that there's a hundred million people out there right now that are racking their brain, trying to figure out the scheme behind the absurdity, trying to figure out why a rock will be here a billion years after we are gone, and it's not necessary, for them, for me, for the sake of conversation, I don't know... one day you'll understand what I did. Just keep in mind what I said about duty to self, and realization of the world as a whole. Okay?"

"Okay." That was our signal. We were done.

"Listen Ester, I'm sorry again, you know, for waking you. Tell mom I said hi and I love her, okay."

"Okay."

I heard a click and then I just sat there listening to the dial tone. It felt so right. The two men had left behind a half of a sleeve of fries, most of it in a pile of ketchup. I thought about eating what was left over, but was afraid of getting full, anything in my stomach would certainly kill off these dreams of implausible rebellion grandeur. I don't know what I was thinking. I *do* know that when I picked up the package of fries, my conscience caught the stare of the Dairy Princess behind the bulletproof glass. Her expression was of an embarrassed teenage girl. She probably thought that I was a homeless vagrant that scored big with a pile of ketchup. Little did she know that I was neither hungry nor without cupboards. She looked away as I picked up the food. My stomach just glanced at it and an urgent shock wave came over me. I could just stuff my face and walk away with no regret. I didn't believe in regret, but just like pride, it came knocking on my door one too many mornings. My life tried to hold much more prominent beliefs, like starving for no reason, like getting beat up for no reason, like getting drunk for no reason, like preaching to strangers about reason for no reason, and of course, proper waste disposal was at the top of the list. I took the trash up to the embarrassed girl without even a splotch of the sweet tomato puree missing. "It must be a real hassle to come out of your castle. This is how plagues begin Miss." I sort of flopped the trash up on the counter. She was completely terrified of me. "I'm sorry." I told her and walked away, keeping my door locked. The smell of the food lingered with me along with the pride and the regret.

    I looked up at the three clouds in the sky and had a vision of hopping a ghost train out of this place, but a sharp pain in my abdomen appropriately interrupted this daydream. It almost put me to my knees. There was a line of oaks swaying in the breeze while bleeding a thick restless sap. I remembered just then how fucked up my face looked. That was the real reason the Dairy Princess was staring at me. "Survive for Christ's sake!" I noticed my voice as I was passing by a woman getting out of her car. I wondered if I always talked to myself out loud, but only noticed it when other people were around.

I went home and gathered some of the greatest masterpieces ever written and put them in a box. Looking over the collection, I figured about four dollars a book. There were twenty-six in all, so I figured a hundred bucks would be in my pocket before the end of the day.

I put the box in Charlie's backseat, and then went in to take a shower. There wasn't any soap in the soap dish, but there was some residue of a cleaning product. My fingernails scraped out the gunk. It was enough. It would have to be. The water seemed to just roll over my body as opposed to hitting it. I couldn't grasp a thought. It killed me to just stand there wet with soap residue in my fingernails staring at the moldy tile wall and all my mind would tell me was *wall*. Even in the midst of drying off when my brain clicked back on, I couldn't quite remember if I had cleaned myself or not. After the shower I decided to take the box by foot. It was probably only two and a half miles, maybe an hour or so walk.

Two hours later, I walked into the store. I was pretty tight with Hans, the owner of Trade Street Used Books. He didn't seem to like that I had arrived with a full box. There were two types of people who stopped into a used bookstore, people who were about to move, and people who were about to stay.

"Hey Hans!" I threw the box on the floor, physically weak, but mentally revived with hope. "Got some good stuff for you." All I could think of was making a world famous chili with my *almost ready* tomatoes. It was the only way I could picture my immortality. Hans said something that bled through my ears and he smiled in such a phony way that he could have either been dying or unsure of who I was. There was a time when I would leave his store with two bags of books. Most of the ones in the box had actually come from Hans. What a great business, recycling wisdom.

"I'm going to browse." I did something with my finger that reminded me of a kid on the Fourth of July. "I'm starting a whole new collection." It wasn't a lie, because my new collection was just going to be one book, and that was new for me. The A-B used literature section started right near the register. It was so typical to start looking there, but it didn't matter because my eyes defied my forehead. I couldn't help but to affectionately look over at my newest saint. Hans went through my books with the intensity of a lunatic hot dog eating champion. He separated them into six piles. I loved Hans, yes, I was in love with Hans. My mind configured the six piles as being dollar amounts from $1 to $6. I breathed easier with my conclusion, and then comfortably browsed through the D section. There was a big goofy hardback of *The Brothers Karamazov* on the top shelf designated for oversized books. As I reached for it, my gut rubbed up against the third shelf. It depressed the hell out of me that a man could go without any food for days and still have a gorgeous beer gut. So I decided to stick with the lower shelves. As I made my way down the alphabet I became paranoid with the thought that maybe my stomach was swollen and not just a portly remnant of booze. My hand pushed into the flesh as if I could finally use all that medical school training. It felt fine, just a little greedy.

I went down to the K section, which was closest to Hans. There was an edition of *One Flew Over the Cuckoo's Nest* that I had never seen, so it was a good time to start a conversation. "Never seen this version of Cuckoo, it's a great cover."

Hans looked up and you could tell he had no idea what I was talking about. "Yes, yes," he admitted to my correctness. "You look almost as bad as you did last time, just a different body part."

"It is true Hans, I have to stop running into walls." I always finished sentences in which I thought were clever with a sharp redneck, "Ha!" But Hans didn't think it was funny. He managed to let me have a grimace though, such a considerate human that Hans.

"It's a good selection huh? It's mostly stuff I got from you, so don't go trying to rip me off." I tried to joke around but...

"Yes, good." He started taking the piles up to the register counter. I looked through Miller, Nabokov, and Plath with a strange warm comfort that everything was going to be like a new light bulb starting that day. Then there was this sigh that lowered the heat. It made me paranoid, so I went back over to the K's. He was flipping through each book and then putting them all in one pile on the floor.

"Everything alright?" I asked as my stomach made a dreadful grumble. He didn't say anything directly to me, but just continued to flip through the books and put them in the same pile. Finally after, I don't know, fifteen books, he put one in a different pile. It was the book that Alex had sent me, and one that I'm ashamed to say I hadn't even opened. It had something to do with this writer in Bunker Hill that was waiting for an Earthquake or something. Maybe he sent it to me because I lived on Bunker Street? Anyway, Hans exhaled and said, "Did you do all of this?" He handed me *Franny and Zooey*.

"Do what?" I looked over a page that had every line highlighted in three different colors. "Oh yeah, have you read this book? This page here is so fucking good! Look, look right here, read this line!" I get really excited when talking about words. I read Salinger's words out loud, "I'm sick of not having the courage to be an absolute nobody." I looked to Hans for a reaction, but he didn't care, no one cared.

"No, no I haven't read it." He ran his fingers through his thick white hair and looked away to the big pile of books. "I can't buy these." He put his hand on the larger pile. There were three books not a part of the rejected. "They have too many highlighted pages. A few is fine, but these, these are ruined." He shrugged.

I became confused, convincing my brain that I couldn't possibly understand what he meant. "No, you see, I bought these from you, they're the same ones."

"The same ones except that they are polluted with one reader's opinion. The words in literature are for each individual's interpretation, not yours wholly, not if you're going to try and sell them or even give them away for that matter." He seemed mad.

"Hans, you have to understand that it's not my opinion, it's like music in movies, it's there to enhance the mood." I dove into desperation. "My highlights actually make the books more valuable." I tugged at the hair on my chin to help me think. "Like critical editions man!"

"I do business sir, only facts, no interpretations, no highlighted books." Then he proceeded to give me his whole business philosophy, but I blanked it out, because my eyes trumped out my other senses. They stared over the dust on the three lone books worthy of someone else's shelf. It made me sad that I hadn't fucked them up like the rest. I snapped out of the daze when Hans mentioned the money. "I'll give you twelve dollars for these three." It wasn't much, but it was a few meals, a little more time on Earth, and most importantly a ten-minute moment of sloth indulgence. I took away the book that Alex had sent me, and held it without explanation. "You see Hans, I walked this box of books over and in my condition it might be impossible to get them back home, so why don't we just settle on a very good price for your side, you know… to help both of us out, an economical justification of sorts.

Now, I believe there are about twenty books left over, so let's just do an extra twenty on top of the twelve."

"The money isn't the point. I just explained that to you, but I'm beginning to think that you do not listen to many people. You can have the twelve dollars for the three books and if you don't want the others, there is a donation box out front that goes to a children's school of literacy. Honestly, I'd rather you not put them in there, but I can't stop you."

What kind of fool did he think was in front of him? Yes, I have several issues that don't fit in with most, but I wouldn't be insulted with lies about charity, especially concerning children. And I have to tell you that I generally believe everyone, but the way he said it, like he was talking through his nose, like the way he crossed his pinky over his ring finger, well, it just didn't sit well with me. I held up the book like I was going to strike him, "I'm keeping this one, how much for the other two?"

Boy, he got scared all of a sudden. It was a simple question. He reached under the counter and nervously laid down $8.50.

"Thanks Hans." I went outside and put the rest of my *ruined* books in the so-called donation box. It was nice to give back to the community and still have a little money to get by. That was all one needed in life anyway, that and a short memory.

The haze of late summer surrounded me. My head was a running faucet. Sometimes I thought that's where all my normal sense leaked out. There was music in the air, the humming of car tires, the beating of construction, the faltering of high heels, the yapping of gangs of toddlers, and the wind, the wind cut through the buildings like God blowing a flute. My poor mind was enlightened to a degree of crumb madness. I didn't want it to stop, but my fingertips in my pockets let me know that food was on its way, and all this record player bliss would run backwards into a slow murmured laughter.

Once again, all of a sudden, that abdominal pain struck me as if I had just swallowed a barrel of acid. There was nothing to do except give in to the sensation. "This is valid God! This!" I yelled and seconds later the internal lightning bolts went away.

There was a grocery store in sight, only a couple snoozes away from my house. I looked through the varieties of Ramen Noodles. With $8.50, I could buy eighty little meals. Before deciding on just ten little meals for a buck, an old acquaintance yelled my name from down the aisle. I knew the voice and turned to see an indifferent expression that was custom-made for me. It was Martin Tours, but everyone just called him Martin. We used to work in the emergency room together. The last time I saw him, he was kicking me out of his house for calling his new girlfriend a cow. He misinterpreted it as meaning bovine-like, fat and such. But now thinking about it, I can't really fathom it meaning anything else. Those days were long gone though, the days where I was preachy and my ego was bigger than my bed. He came toward me.

Martin shook my hand firmly with a joyful sloppiness. It seemed all was forgotten. "Amy and I just got engaged." He told me before anything important. I must have had a surprised mouth, for I didn't respond. "Yeah, I got rid of the cow." He laughed.

"Guilty." My head was spinning. I hadn't spoken to any of my old friends, that is, Martin's friends, in years. It made me frazzled to even imagine them still sitting around eating and getting married.

"Well, forget it..." He started to say something, hesitated, and then started again.

"We're having a small get-together at the house. You should come by."

"Oh, I'm on foot these days." I waited for him to ask why, but he didn't. "I'm doing my duty to save the whales and kangaroos and such."

There was an awkward silence. "Do you want to come with me?" He asked with a regretful tone.

"Oh no, no thank you, I couldn't, there are a million things I have to do."

"Okay, well, I'll get in touch with you soon." He almost cut me off with his response. Boy, that pissed me off. He hoped that I'd just say no and we'd see each other in another year or never. I decided to put off those million things in order to see the old gang. "You know what, I'll do those things tomorrow. Let me grab some beer and we'll go."

I could see the discomfort creep into his body. I would be like a celebrity at his party. Everyone would expect me to say something stupid or at least say a thousand nonsensical, seemingly intelligent things until they wanted to strangle me, but I decided to be surprisingly normal, shock them in a new way. I went over to the beer aisle and grabbed two 40-ouncers. "700 calories a piece!" I showed Martin, but he had already decided to not understand me.

We pulled up to the old dilapidated house that sat back in the dark woods by a small pond. I got a big lump in my throat from nervousness. The people inside would all pretend to be nice to me, and bless their hearts, they try like hell to get into heaven. There wasn't any reason for them to be nice to me, except in the case of them finally realizing that life might not be exactly what they thought it was, and that just because they were drugged with specific morals doesn't necessarily mean that they are right in their judgments. But that happening would be right after one of them stopped to let the wind go by. Martin went in before me and probably cushioned the surprise. I stayed outside and played with the five dogs. They attacked me with their paws and tongues. I understand dogs. They fuck, shit, and sleep. Man was just a fleshy ball of logic surrounded by unreason.

My old buddy Tom came outside to witness the joker rolling around on the ground. The smallest of the pack had gotten a hold of my shirt and was ripping a hole in the sleeve. "I came to invite you in properly, but that's not going to happen." Tom sarcastically said. Tom was a painter and understood chaos better than anyone else in that house.

"Now Tom, I want you to know that life isn't all scissors and glue."

He laughed downhill and then hugged me despite the dog saliva. It felt really good to have someone's arms around me. I didn't want him to let go. We went inside, and everyone - everyone being my old roommate Steve, Tom's girl Irene, Martin's soon-to-be-wife Amy, Robert my unwritten nemesis, and others turned to flash their phony smiles. It was nice to be back among all the familiar faces, to be a part of the gang again. The great thing about Martin's parties was that he passed out distractions like a bowl of mints. There was a foosball table, ping-pong, video games, bong hits, full keg system, dogs, a poker/blackjack table, and a TV in every room. I opened the 40-ounce and let the warm liquid splash down on my empty stomach. Since all these guys saw each other every day, they had nothing new to talk about except my random presence. The stories of my supposed antics came from every corner of the room.

"Remember that concert we went to, and you kept walking off from us, and I was like, that motherfucker can stay here!" Irene said. It was obviously her first experience with someone getting really excited about music.

"I go into my own world when music gets inside me, I can't help it." I said apologetically, because I was there to be normal that night.

"Yeah, we were in the car, probably seconds away from leaving you," Tom said. "But here comes this idiot stumbling, running through a field beside the parking lot, still way overexcited about the show, which pissed us off even more." Some of the guys laughed. Irene shot me a look of detestable expectation. I looked away trying to remember if I had done something horrible to her. Nothing was coming to the surface. I was just different than them, nothing else, but a little difference in some places could be seen as a man dressed up in a devil suit with a pitchfork penis.

"It seemed like we all had a great time." I said. "Shit, I didn't even know until months later that you guys were pissed at me. You should have just kicked the shit out of me right then. I can't stay mad at anyone for more than two seconds."

"What happened to your nose then?" A stranger with a lump of tobacco inside his lip asked me.

"My nose is a byproduct of duty, not anger." It caused a slight pause in thought, but no one responded.

"Alright, what about the time at Harry's Saloon? When you turned over the table full of beers and grabbed the waiter like you were going to kill him." Steve asked.

"I'm pretty sure that was in the confines of two seconds." I told them jokingly, but I really only knew the story from them telling me about it. Everyone was able to laugh at it that night, but before they hated me, they talked shit about me, complained about me, and while sitting there with my beer, dizzy, listening to the stories, I felt like telling them how boring their lives would have been back then if I didn't go outside the boundaries. But I didn't. It seemed too systematic. It was just as phony as anything. I just needed to be myself. Let them tell stories in between bong hits and baseball games.

I finished the first bottle and didn't feel so hot. The stories were still going, but I wasn't paying attention any longer. Actually, what happened, was instead of hearing each person talking, I could hear all the different conversations together. I tried to concentrate on one thing, but it just didn't work. "...the shot counts if it hits another player... pass me that ashtray... that's the first of the plugs... you filled me with no warning... remember that?... they're from Scotland... remember that?... don't go in there for another... remember that time you tried to steal that keg off that back patio?" Steve was looking at me, but someone else said something. I wasn't sure if he was talking about me. I was pretty certain that it wasn't me. I didn't have anything against stealing, but that just wasn't my kind of work. "My work was much more of a victim of being useless in a society that demands results. I'd steal stationary just to write the proprietor and let them know that there were real thieves out there that stole bricks from your house and pennies from your paycheck. It's about going home, going back to the womb. Staying away from bringing things with us. Tasks! Tasks make me sick. Bringing home the bacon, the woman, a smile for empty souls begging to be filled. The safeguards, the walls of time. The places that hold trophies and pictures." I realized as the clock struck nothing, and as time and my old friends stood blankly staring at me, that I had let my thoughts get out of my head. It was as if another one of the gods of mercy decided to raid my freezer and tell everyone what I was trying to save for the cold season. I think I had been spending too much time by myself. I probably did this all the time, but didn't have to worry about my walls judging. They all turned away and I could hear their thoughts, their judgments, their fear stabbing me in the sides.

"You alright?" Tom asked, knowing the answer.

They seemed to be as confused as me. "Of course! There has never been one time in my life in which I have never been alright, as opposed to contrary thought." Ah ha! I was back. They thought I was going to be normal, well, it was time to give them one more patch for their goddamn story quilts. "You know, if we die right now, it would be the same as if we died yesterday, when we were born, or a hundred years from now. How do you feel about that?" I asked the room, but all eyes avoided mine. I caught Steve, and he smiled at my transformation. He was probably so happy that he didn't live with me any longer. His wry smile was the only product available. The only ones who weren't concerned with my rants were captivated by the television. "Just the same! Your reaction is just as useless as your non-reaction. It's too late for you to conquer complacency. Too late for you to care whether you actually did anything worthwhile in this world!" I went over to the TV watchers and grabbed one of their cigarettes off the coffee table. "I'm going to hang with the dogs. They are at least, at minimum, honest."

Three of the dogs came up to me less aggressively than the first time. The other two stayed on the ground. It wasn't the same as a stranger arriving. After a few drags of the cigarette, the other three got bored and went away. I was really going to try and fit in for the whole night, but it just didn't happen like it always never happened. The problem with people like me is that we don't allow any room for weakness in others. Humans have to be weak in order to survive. We would much rather find ways to adapt than to overcome or fix the root. So that's what I did. I adapted to the situation instead of trying to fix my old friends.

Everyone had gone back to their distractions. I grabbed a can of beer from the kitchen and joined Martin and Robert's conversation. They were talking about baseball, something I could ease into. "No man. Greatest ever? Greatest right now maybe, but of all time, no chance in hell." Martin debated. I had my own opinions, but a bowl of tortilla chips and a bottom layer of dried salsa caught my attention. My stomach created a sharp pain to tell my brain to advance my feet in the direction of food, but fruitless pride was as big as oxygen. I will get food of my own accord, I thought, while looking for the calorie count on the can of beer.

"His defense, then his consistent home runs at bat, like every twelve I think-"

"One-forty-five!" I laughed, reading the calories on the can. They looked at me in question.

"What?" Martin questioned.

"One-hundred and forty-five runs batted in last season if I'm not mistaken." I said with delight. My clever cover-up of my insanity was the wine cellar of all virtuous faults.

"I thought it was 154?" Robert replied quite unsure.

"Perhaps. Perhaps you're just making up things, but perhaps you are right." I walked away, back to the playroom. There was a blunt being passed around. Tom yelled at me while holding it out in my direction. "Hit this you crazy bastard!" He hit the nail on the head, but I didn't smoke weed, it made me weird. I took the soggy roach. It was easy to inhale despite the remaining saliva, and I became instantly lightheaded. The couch called me over. Irene was a big fan of mine. She thought I was a despicable animal that shit and pissed where I wanted. I thought that I could take her right then, show her what kind of animal I was. I laughed out loud. She turned to me quickly, ready to judge. "What's so funny?"

"All of us putting on a show, actors perfecting our craft, waiting on the tears, the hate, the sex, and waiting for me, the jester to make you forget that normalcy that has crept on to your stage! That is what is so goddamn funny!"

"So what are you waiting for?" She was so cold. "Make us feel something for once!"

"That is the tragedy, I'm just being normal tonight, I'm watching your TV, smoking your weed, drinking your beer, playing your games, and we will all wake up tomorrow with the same hangover, and then, only then, will I wander off beyond the fence. But I'll sleep well tonight knowing that my headache will be yours." I held up my can for her to cheers me, but she chose to ignore me. I finished my beer and the dizziness went away. There was an acoustic guitar over in the corner by the bar. I felt pretty goddamn musical at that moment. To say that the music was in me would be an understatement. I didn't really know how to play, but I did know how to press my fingers against the fret board and strum like there was no tomorrow. I started lightly in order to get my vision down. The song was the ending to many rock and roll songs, like when everyone is going crazy on their instruments right before they all halt at the same moment. Who knows how long I practiced this ending, but I do know that the longer I played, the louder the instrument sounded. It was uncanny. The loyal crowd began to move away from the melodic mess into the other rooms and outside. Like a man who not only had to, but *needed* to finish his show, I played on. Finally, someone came over to put an end to the noise. Martin grabbed my arms and yelled, "Stop! For God's sake stop!" He said like I wasn't ever going to stop, but I would've, and I did.

"For God's sake? The bible says make a joyful noise unto the lord." I smiled.

"You've ruined my guitar!" I looked down and there was blood everywhere, on the strings, my fingers, my legs, everywhere. It didn't make any sense.

"What happened?" I asked him.

"Dude, you have to go."

"Don't you see man?" I held up my bloody fingers. "Something higher took control of me. You just witnessed some spiritual madness." I think I was kidding around, but like I said, weed makes me weird.

"I'm not sure what that was, but it was just like every other time you come around. I thought you had grown up man." Martin was so disappointed. He followed me to the kitchen where I washed my hands. I was calm, actually feeling pretty good. The water stung. Martin handed me some paper towels. "Hold on, I'll get you some bandages."

"I love you Martin." I really did, no joke. I loved all those guys. They were really great people, really amazing. They were on a level that would forever be impossible for me to reach. While Martin was gone I thought it would be a good time to eat. The bowl of chips and salsa was still there. I poured the little broken chips over the dried tomatoes and then ran a few drops of water over it, just to bring it back to life. When Martin came back I was scooping the mix into my mouth guiltily and with a determined pleasure. He shook his head and put the first-aid kit down on the dirty counter. The salsa began to burn the little cuts on my fingers so I ran water over them again. Martin was about to lose it. Even a crazy bastard like me could see that. So I grabbed my second 40-ounce beer and prepared to leave. The rest of the party hid from my departure. They had all miraculously disappeared. I hugged Martin. "Thanks for inviting me over. Give me a call sometime, we'll hang out." The joke was on him, my phone didn't work. Upon leaving, the dogs sort of followed me up the driveway. I picked up a stick and teased them. I threw it up the gravel road hoping they would come with me. The dogs just watched it crash to the ground and then turned back toward their home. I was on my own again.

I opened the beer and headed toward home. It was probably three to five miles, but my nerves jumped with excitement. It was sort of nice to be around friends again. I had been alone for months, not including Floyd and Floyd's wife. The walk on the road from Martin's house was almost pitch black. Hookers, junkies, and dealers used it to hide and to survive. They were my people, nothing more than bottom feeders living one trick or shot or deal at a time. There was a parked car under the overhang of some tree limbs. A man was sitting in the driver's seat while another person appeared to be going down on him. They didn't notice me right beside the window. This scene did not make me sick, but either way I bent over and puked out the chips and salsa. My digestive system didn't know what to do with it. I washed my mouth out with beer and kept moving.

About 35 ounces of beer later I was getting close to home. I had to stop every few minutes because of those same pains that shot through my stomach. God and the devil had some weird bet going on. The pot must have been huge, big stakes, like a million innocent men in prison, bigger than guilt, something from thousands of years ago when fear was invented, when there were burning bushes, worldwide floods, and water into wine. I couldn't wait to see who won. My body was as weak as ever. I desperately needed food and sleep, but a higher power pushed me on. It seemed so obvious when it showed itself. I took a different route home, a way I hadn't been in about a year. There was a forgotten cemetery hidden at a dead-end road. The ground was dry. It hadn't rained in days, since before the coma. There were fresh flowers everywhere. It had to be a Saturday or a Sunday or maybe a Monday, that's when the flowers were in abundance. Once I was near the middle of the small field of gravestones, I felt like I was supposed to die right then. Another sharp pain made me double over. The almost empty bottle rolled over T.J. Davis's little patch of paradise. He had lived for seventy-eight years, over double my life. I couldn't imagine doing this for another forty or fifty-something years. This is when I was sure the end was close. I knew it would be over soon even if I lived to a hundred. It seemed as if something in me had given up. Everything became dull, silent, and peaceful. My blissful unmotivated mind took an interest in Mr. Davis's flowers. They were white and yellow daisies mixed with pink carnations. I reached over and began plucking the petals off the daisies. I don't remember what they tasted like, but I do know that I felt significantly better for each flower I ate. So much better in fact, that I crawled over to the next metal vase and ate Mr. and Mrs. Newlove's flowers. My appetite for these flowers became insatiable. I crawled from one grave to the next in ecstasy. My senses began to act as if an amplifier were connected to every little nerve, taste bud, and canal. For each set of flowers I ate, I said a prayer for the dead and their family. "Oh God, bless the wind and the souls that turn the world, and bless us fools that think we can outlast you, that will always ignore you, that will always turn to you when confused. Give us faith lord to forget we invented you. Amen. Oh yes, and help the families of the dead forget that flowers are just for recycling, just like we are just for recycling."

Before going home and right before the sun was about to come up, I pissed on the next grave. It reminded me of a story that Alex wrote. It was about these aliens that urinated out of their palms, and it smelled like cinnamon buns because that's all they ate on Earth. Humans couldn't wait for them to piss all over the streets, and they couldn't wait to shake their hands afterward. So pissing on the grave didn't bother me because I knew it smelled like pink carnations.

the epitome of the torturous fatal counterfeit...

Day 12,303

Even the clang of my mailbox couldn't make me run out into the new day. A single ray of sunshine revealed the mass of dust in the air. My body was so weak that I couldn't even get out of bed. If only I had a cup of water or just anything that was normal to put in one's body. There was that stick of butter in the fridge. Maybe I could bang on the wall and ask Floyd's wife for some bread. Nothing would move though, just the explosions in my head. Maybe those flowers were poisonous? I was in paralysis. Eating the dead's flowers? This is what I deserve, to die in shame right in between those dirty sheets, by myself, no one to wonder what they would inherit from my vast fortune.

I dozed back off at some point in the paranoia, and had another nightmare. I was trying to sleep on this bed of gold coins, but kept turning over and repositioning myself. The coins would conform to my body, but they were cold and hard, and they covered my eyes. I woke from the nightmare and something was irritating my hip. My bandaged fingers reached down in my pocket and found two quarters. I jumped up as if the paralysis was just a figment of my imagination. I had forgotten all about the money left over from the two 40oz meals. There were four crumpled up dollar bills in my other pocket. That was all I needed, a new day, the day in which life would turn around for me. God was giving me a boost even though I didn't deserve it. There was going to be no screwing around this time. I would only buy food, get my energy back and start up this new life, this new chance that we all take for granted.

I decided to take Charlie to the grocery store. My legs didn't have the energy to walk. I sat down in the worn-out bucket seat, breathed in the odor of road dust, put in the key, and turned the ignition switch only to hear a clicking sound. The battery was dead. I cursed myself. It had been months since I had started the old girl up. We had been dying together, a regular modern day Romeo and Juliet. So instead of the grocery store, I walked up to the convenience store, only five blocks away. I floundered around the glowing aisles, stopping and staring at every little processed gem, figuring out what I could get for my $4.50. There was a can of chili that reminded me of my tomatoes. One day soon I would be able to pick off the fruit and eat for a week straight, live off the land, right out of the dirt. There was the farmer, the stocker, the writer, the accountant, the musician, the bum, the boss, the juicer, the athlete, and the never-ending list of ego-protein sludge waiting to figure out what kind of waste we really were. How we played along with the universe. He never thought that we'd learn math and make up words for infinity. He never thought that we'd actually invent mass produced paper that would take his place at the table of worship. The epitome of the torturous fatal counterfeit. One would have to think that a reedy smile of satisfaction must be secretly hidden behind the God of the stars mighty reverence and compassion.

    I bought a loaf of bread, the can of chili, a candy bar, some square ham slices, and a can of tuna. The clerk handed me back thirty-nine cents and it brought tears to my eyes.

    I went outside and sat on the curb. I tore open the candy bar wrapper and bit into the chocolate. It made my head spin, but in a good way. I put my hands up in the air as if I had just won a race. A young girl in the back seat of a car was staring at me. Her dad was pumping gas and smoking a cigarette. I waved at her, like waving goodbye, because I could picture the whole car going up in flames. She flipped me off like she just learned how to perform the crude act. I remember as a kid when the older boy next door taught me how to flip someone off. He held my fingers down and pulled the middle one up and said, "This means you hate the person you show it to." I asked him why, and he said, "Because it's the finger you put inside a girl. It means fuck you." Of course this wasn't true, but when told at the impressionable age of seven it sticks with you for life. I learned an alternate theory later on that it was a gesture that originated in medieval times. When archers were captured the enemy would cut off their bow-pulling finger, the middle finger. So when they would show the enemy their middle finger it was like saying, 'Hey motherfucker I got my trigger!' Don't even get me started about where the word 'motherfucker' originated.

    I continued to stare at the girl flipping me off until she grew bored of taunting me. These days staring at someone is much more offensive than showing a stupid finger that doesn't shoot bow and arrows any longer.

    Up above, little patches of puffy clouds stood still in the sky. In between the clouds, streaks of the blue universe formed beams of validation. Several legs passed by me. I smiled. One could hardly guess why I would be happy all of a sudden, but definitely at some point between those clouds, one could understand why there is so much to die for.

Part 2

all those wasted hours out there moving branches and rocks, pretending to push a boulder up a mountain…

Day 12,304

The next day I was out by my tomato plants, not nearly as interested in them as usual. Ham sandwiches tend to create this distraction, that is, make you forget about the importance of tomatoes. I was working on a poem about a drug that gives you complete faith in whatever higher power you choose, but the only problem was that so many humans couldn't function without fear. I was thinking about ending the poem with a mass suicide, since everyone on the drug truly believed that they would go to heaven if they asked God for forgiveness of their sins. It turns out people found it difficult to reason with life as a contradiction. It was a work in progress.

There was an annoying humming sound coming from the other side of the fence that made me put the pen down. Floyd's wife was doing something useless again. The day was amazing up until then. All it took was one happy animal let loose out of her cage to shit all over the Sistine Chapel. My strength was almost back and my mind was as clear as it had been in weeks. I left my plants to go and put a stop to this contempt of windows once and for all.

She saw me coming, but didn't acknowledge it. "Now Floyd's wife, there must be certain days in a person's life in which they step outside their front door and see, well, a clump of weeds, or a dry lawn, or even hell, a full mailbox, and they don't turn into a damn ice cream truck or something." I said, but she didn't hear a goddamn word.

"Floyd was going on last night about that list he gave you." She was pruning a piece of grass or something. "He thinks maybe you lost it. He says you're the kind of person that would take a list like that and roll up marijuana in it, and I said *Floyd*! And he just laughed, which means he was pulling my leg, but he really does think you lost the list." She looked up for the first time. She had one of those silly straw yard hats on. The kind that old women wear to make the neighbors think they have a goddamn green thumb or something. I had no idea what she was talking about.

"What list?"

Floyd's wife looked at me strangely. "The list. The one with all the chores on it for the Corinth property."

"Corinth?" Could she be fucking with me? Did she have this capacity?

"Corinth, the place you supposedly go everyday to stay in our house for free. Floyd was right. Floyd is very, um, very perceptive about things like that. He said he knows you are a good worker, just your head's not all there, not completely screwed on." She laughed. "He said you got leaks!" Boy, that cracked her up.

Now, if I wasn't so confused about this supposed list, I would take offense to this goddamn hag telling me that I was a hard-working retard. "Oh, that list, of course, of course, I've got that list." I still had no idea. "I was thinking of the movies, the movie list."

"Well okay. I'll let him know. He said he was going to make another copy for you cause he knew you lost it somewhere."

This was a rare situation in which I wasn't drunk, or delusional, or angry, or hungry, or anything. I just existed in the upright form. I knew that my life would be easier if I'd just tell her the truth that it would be best if Floyd make me another list just in case I misplaced it, but, "Tell Floyd not to be silly, the list is as good as done."

She looked at me as if I had a bluebird on my shoulder, and then she went back to humming.

"That's a *nice* tune Floyd's wife, have a *nice* day." I went inside and began to look for this so-called list. It was probably in one of those stupid books I gave away. It was as good as any day to organize my things anyway. Maybe get some more books together for Hans to turn down. I don't think I owned a book that wasn't full of revelations in the form of yellow highlighted smears and black squiggly lines. I looked around the cozy apartment and had a whim to just get rid of everything once and for all. Of course the exception was the treasures decorating the walls. All I needed was a good floor, a couple pieces of wood over my head, and the scraps of life on my walls. There was a postcard of Neal Cassidy and Jack Kerouac above a picture of Alex and me. There was a picture of my dad holding my sister. There was a poem from Bukowski about rolling the dice. There was everything that meant anything up in front of me.

I put together another box of novels, looking through them and separating the less highlighted from the others. All of my important documents were hidden in my favorite books, but the list was nowhere to be found. The only other place it would be was in a pile of papers and mail that had been rotting beside the door. I sat on the floor and spread it all out. The pile was impressive. It must have been over a month's worth of fire starter. I only opened letters from friends and family and those didn't come too often. After a few minutes I pulled out a blank envelope that wasn't mail. It was in my mailbox at least twenty days ago. I remember looking it over for about two seconds and then throwing it in the *disregard* pile. The second time around, I actually opened it. Sure enough, it was Floyd's list. My heart sank as my eyes read in disbelief the things I was supposed to have done already. It was just about everything that I hadn't done. I was already twenty, twenty-five hours behind, maybe more, but with this new information, maybe sixty, maybe a hundred?

    I panicked. The day must have been halfway over. I put on my work clothes and literally ran out the door. It was time to stop fucking around. My mind raced with anxiety, all those wasted hours out there moving branches and rocks, pretending to push a boulder up a mountain. I was just like them, typing up a speech, pulling weeds, building roads, and pumping gas. I calmed myself at the bus stop by pacing the sidewalk and repeating, "Just ten minutes at a time." Several people passed me with their eyes distant. They didn't want to disturb me. Even the birds flew by silently, not looking down, not touching down.

"Excuse me, do you have the time?" I asked a man sweating underneath his tie.

"No." He looked away.

"You have a watch on."

He kept on walking. It was such a waste of time, reminding myself about time. Down Central Avenue was a clear view of the Arcane city skyline. This was one of the few streets in the city that wasn't lined with towering trees and voter signs. I was sort of in love with this place, but the kind of love in which one knew that it would have to end tragically.

HAPPINESS IS GIVING HOPE. Sign Guy was sleeping against a telephone pole, using his sign as shade. His ragged top hat was on its side and out in front of him, probably empty except all the hope it possessed.

The bus picked me up and dropped me off thirty minutes later. It was uneventful. That was my new resolution, to make my life more uneventful, at least for a while. It felt so late out, even though it couldn't have been past five. I stopped into the bait shop with my thirty-nine cents. I needed to prove my sanity while it was still available. My lovely pink-lipped clerk wasn't behind the register. There was a younger gal that had never seen me before. It was nice to get fresh opportunities with people, first impressions and all that bullshit.

"How are you?" I never asked that. It's such a stupid question. How are you? It's mostly stupid because the person asking doesn't really care, and also because the person asking always repeats what the other said. Like this time:

"I'm great, you?" The girl said, in what I thought might be a northern accent.

"I'm great." I laughed to myself because I wasn't the fool. "Are you new? I haven't seen you before."

"You buy a lot of worms?"

"No… the other things..." I drew a blank.

"Lottery tickets?" She asked sincerely. The only other answer was cigarettes.

"That's funny."

She looked at me strangely. She wasn't being funny.

"There are two types of miserable people in this world, ones that buy lottery tickets, and ones that sell them." I regretted saying that.

"You got me pegged, I do both." Her sense of humor wasn't from the South.

"But you said you were doing great?"

"You did too. Are you really?" She had long curly black hair that landed in her mouth when she tilted her head. Between that and her voice, I danced without moving.

"Yeah, I really *am* great, whatever that means." I fiddled with a bucket of lighters on the counter. "You're not from here?"

"I fell from up there." She pointed in the direction of what she assumed was north.

It was quite confusing. "So you decided to come down south to work in a bait shop? That's weird."

"Thank God someone finally said that. Everyone else just acts like it's normal or whatever."

"It's not."

"Yes, you don't have to keep emphasizing it." She laughed very throaty. It was wonderful, unbridled. "My parents divorced a few years ago and my mom moved down to the lake… then things got a bit uncomfortable for me up in Michigan, so to speak, so I ran away from myself, and..." She stopped talking and looked toward the door. Two men came in. "I almost forgot I was at work. What can I get for you?"

The only reason I was there was to prove my sanity and I think the task had been accomplished. It was just the wrong clerk. But either way, I didn't want to stop talking to her. There were some twenty-five cent packs of gum at the counter. "Actually, just some gum, it helps me work."

She rang it in. I pretended to only have large bills in my pocket. "Oh wait, I may have some change, oh yes, here we are."

"What does the gum help you do?"

"Oh, I'm a lumberjack." Goddamn, I was one witty bastard.

She laughed that beautiful girlish chokehold laugh. "Really?"

"Yep, I'm Paul, Paul Bunyan." This was my test of intelligence or at the very least, random folklore.

"Then I must be Babe." She came through.

"I have to say, for a blue ox, you're doing well." I lost it. I could only be smooth for about two seconds. "I mean, you're not like an ox, you're pretty, is what I mean."

"Thank you." She blushed. "You actually make a pretty good lumberjack. The scruff is good, but a full beard would be better, and an orange beanie would help."

"And denim overalls?"

"Yes!"

The men were ready to check out and they didn't seem to have time to watch me flirt. "Okay, well thanks for the gum."

"I didn't make it, I just took your money."

I walked out with a smile, feeling like God had just blew me. My feet were confused on which way to go. I knew that there was an urgency to close the situation before my real self came out again. I went back into the store. "I'm going to show you around this God-awful place."

"Are you always this psycho?" She was ringing up a six-pack and cigarettes.

"I'm usually worse."

She laughed without looking at me. "Okay then," She pushed the paper bag forward. "$8.68 please." She took the customer's money and slowly gave him change as if she was trying to torture me. The customers left the store. She took an apple and bit into it while staring at me, maybe sizing me up. "Friday, at eight, come pick me up here."

The demand echoed through my mind and almost got lost. "If you insist." I told her and waved goodbye. Once outside I started to run in full stride. It was a solid mile or so to my destination. It could have been ten miles and I would have run them all, nothing could bother me. I even ran right by Willie's house with a smile. He wasn't out in the yard so he must have been passed out already, exhausted from being so damn brilliant. I reminded myself that everything was valid, even Willie. There was no reason to be bitter about anyone or anything. My life was finally starting to come together. The universe works in cycles for the fortunate. I've been waiting for my stars to align for such a long time, and when they finally do, it'll be a hundred times better than paying an assistant to do it for me. I sat on a stump in the woods and began to cry while out of breath. I hated when life made me emotional. "That's one for the devil! Lost angel of heaven!" The words just came out. My biblical subconscious. I'm not sure what it meant.

It was beginning to get dark. I pulled out the list and tried to find a short task, something to get a feeling of completion, something to fit in with the glorious day. My mind raced with the possibilities of Babe the blue ox beside me. A good woman could really straighten a man up. A good strong woman was the only being that could bring me to my knees and ruin me for a lifetime. I imagined the smell of her hair, the smell of her cunt. I thought about how she would feel, sweaty and collapsed against my chest. Then my daydream was washed away by a singular female necessity… goddamn money. And then I couldn't for the life of me figure out when Friday was. For once, I wished to be walking down a mountain, following a slow-moving boulder, taking in perspective, finding absurdity and laughing at it. But it seemed that my life was pushing the rock up the mountain, up Everest. Maybe even something higher? Mt. Olympus? So high that I finally meet Zeus face to face.

One of the tasks on the list was to move any large rocks to the property line in order to form a wall. It seemed appropriate. Here I come Zeus, here I come God, here I come Babe the blue ox.

they grew angry, and beat him for waking forgotten longings in their heads...

Day 12,305

In the morning, or what I assumed to be a morning feel, my anticipation of duty made me want to get out of bed. I didn't. There were so many things to do, find out what day it was, figure out how to get a little money, somehow get Charlie back to life, write a poem for my beautiful blue ox, and then try to get in a ten-hour day in the woods. Floyd's alarm went off. I wondered which one of the four times it was. He slapped off the obnoxious talk show. The blanket was up to my nose. It was a brilliant concept, talk radio, not the blanket. It eased the waking mind into a sleepwalk mentality of getting away from wanting to think. Our minds could focus on the future and all that other stuff that gives us a reason to forget the present. It was still silent. I was on edge, waiting for noise. "Maybe the geniuses will tell me the day and the weather." My musty breath laughed inside my blanket. "They grew angry, and beat him for waking forgotten longings in their heads..." I tried to remember the line from Yeats, but apparently dozed back off.

The alarm went off again and woke me from the sleepy poem. I jumped out of the bed and yawned like never before. There was a little bread left. I made a grilled cheese sandwich without the cheese, washed it down with tap water without the glass, and then went outside to catch Floyd on his first cigarette. He was just lighting up.

"Morning"

"Heard you lost the list. I can make you another." He told me right out.

"No, no, I have the list. Thank you though."

"Well what the fuck have you been doing out there?" He sounded mad. Maybe it was just the promise of a new day? Maybe Floyd's wife didn't cook him breakfast or give him a hand job or something?

"Improvising, it's what I do best. Structure, lists, and such aren't for me."

Floyd shook his head. I'm pretty sure he didn't care. The work was just a gesture of neighborly philanthropy. "You know one day your shit is going to be on the street when you get home and I'm going to get someone who actually pays money for rent."

The joke was on him; I didn't have any shit. "Hey Floyd, what's the day?"

"Wednesday."

"No the date, of course it's Wednesday."

He looked at me with a curled lip and squinted eyes. Sometimes you just took for granted that you were fooling people. He finished his smoke break, and told me, "Those are going to be some fine tomatoes back there. Another nine or ten days and they'll be perfect."

Ten days? That was impossible! I went to the backyard to look over my green and red fruit. My judgment was five or six days, but I was an amateur at these things, like everything else. It was as if I'd never be a professional anything. Maybe a professional buffoon?

Inside my bedroom I pondered over which possessions to give back to the world. It was necessary to get as much money as possible, because every time a vagina comes into my life, I am forced to go all out. It has a power that is greater than love or art. God didn't fuck that up.

That first edition set of *The Rosy Crucifixion* was calling me, but that would have to be the last item sold. My CDs would have to suffice this time. There were over a hundred in a box. The biggest problem would be getting them there before ten o'clock.

But first things first… work.

When the bus dropped me off I couldn't contain myself. The bait shop teased me from across the street. I contemplated with my temporary reason. 'You already have a date, if you go in now, you can only ruin it.' So I went through the door, not noticing the pink stained cigarette butts out in the parking lot. She recognized me right away. I beat her to her own reaction. "Now listen, I've come to apologize for that incident the other day." I didn't come to do that at all. Why would I make up apologies? "It seems I was wrong, and I beg of your forgiveness."

She looked at me blankly. "I'm not sure what you mean?" She was playing my game against me. How dare the dirty whore!

I fumbled my words. "The other day, the peanut butter, the extra change, the dance request."

She shook her head. "You must be thinking of someone else."

What in the hell was she doing? "What are you trying to pull? You have nothing better to do in your life but make up lies, torture good honest people who are just trying to survive and keep straight in this already fucked up world!"

"Sir, please lower your voice, are you going to buy anything?" She hid her laughter behind her smoke-filled veins.

"Goddamn right I'm going to buy something! I'm going to buy..." I was stuck, because all of a sudden I wasn't sure if she was the same woman. It was too late to turn back though. "Are you telling me that you will denounce the words I gave you, my heart, my poetry, that I... bequeathed unto you!" I pointed a beef jerky stick at her. I don't know how that ended up in my hand. She smiled in a fake polite way. I wanted to kill her. I imagined my hands around her throat, her smile turning to fear.

"Sir you have to buy something or get out."

Those words rang in my head all the way out to the woods. *Buy something* or get out. Buy something *or get out*. I worked like a madman that day, from ten in the morning to ten at night. I carried these mini boulders out of the woods until a wall was built across the border of the property. Even though it was dark you could see the white stones glowing alongside the road. Whenever a car's headlights would come along, the wall could be seen all the way to the horizon. It was a proud day in my life. I create, so I defy. *Buy something or get out!*

put a chainsaw in a man's hands and he thinks he's God all of a sudden...

Day 12,306

My stomach was making those old familiar sounds. I went over to the fridge, opened it, looked back into the empty corners, closed the door, walked over to put my sneakers on, went back to the fridge, and stared inside it again. It was amazingly the same as before, the bottle of Champagne and a pat of butter. I made another breakfast of grilled butter bread and headed out into the day. The bread set on my stomach like splintered wood. I had spoiled it with real food and all of a sudden it had become picky.

At the bus stop a familiar face approached me. It was the man I gave the job reference, obviously coming to thank me. "You know what, you are a fool! Didn't you know that they didn't want an old black man working for them, didn't you know that the time you were wasting was time I could have been looking a for a real job. And I know your name ain't Luke. Luke was there! And I know also, that you were the one who called us sheep that day! So what you got to say for yourself now?"

I'm pretty sure that wasn't a thank you. So I responded like any man with pride, dignity, morals, and such. "I'm sorry, have we met before?"

"Ahhh!" He almost laughed, I think. Then he gave a half-air jab at me, but acted as if I wasn't worth the trouble, which is true for most people. The man walked over to the Dairy Queen benches.

"You do look slightly familiar." I followed him over. "I seem to recall you in a larger shirt." Boy, I could crack myself up. He ignored me. I sat beside him and pointed at Sign Guy. "See that man in the tuxedo over there? That's my best friend. He's the one, he's the one that has it all figured out." His sign read: SMILE AT THE WORLD AND IT WILL SMILE BACK. I smiled at my newest friend and anyone could tell he wanted to hit me. The bus came and we sat at opposite ends, me in the back and him all the way up by the driver. I felt sort of bad, because he seemed depleted, and the last thing he needed was a professional buffoon putting the last nail in his coffin. But on the positive side, the confrontation seemed to settle my stomach. Maybe I should drop by the club and see if they still needed a barman? It was weird that he said they didn't want an old black man, considering the owners were old black men. Oh well, sometimes you can't question the scheme on any level. I was the original candidate and perhaps they didn't even know that I was the one who sent the man. Strategy engulfed my mind. I went up to my old black friend. "Excuse me sir. I must apologize for my behavior. I *was* the one who sent you to the bar, but you have to believe me, it was all with the best intentions. I gave up my spot so you could have a happier life. Now, I will not debate that I am a fool, because it is the story of my life." I paused to let him groan in agreement. "So when you went to the bar, was there someone named Abdiel?"

"Hell no, they laughed at me when I mentioned that stupid name!"

"What about Big John?"

"There was a big mo-fo there, probably named John. Shit, I don't know, I don't even know why I am talking to you or why you think you can talk to me."

"Yes, yes, it is true, but I did try to commit an act of human kindness, and I was wondering if you could answer a quick question?" He didn't respond so I just continued. "Did they ask anything about me, what I looked like, or why you were there, or did you tell them anything at all?"

He looked at me with contempt. "After they laughed about the Abdiel shit, I told them Luke sent me for a bar job, and they said that's Luke, some white boy behind the bar. Luke said he didn't know me. I knew that I had been fooled, so I told them I got the wrong information, and I asked that big mo-fo if they needed a barman anyway. He said he didn't hire black people, especially old black people, so I left." There was a short silence. He looked down at the rubber floor. I stared through the window behind him. "Now isn't Big John, the big mo-fo, black also?" I asked him and he just gave me an agreeing grunt. I went back to the window. There were so many stories repeating as the bus bounced down the road. So many people acting out their roles with no questions asked. "You don't have the classifieds today." I commented to my new friend. He was holding a brown paper bag, one that might contain a sandwich, an apple, and maybe a brownie.

"No, I don't need it."

"You found another job?"

"That's right. After I left that uppity club of yours, I started to think how my plans of the day had been ruined, so I just started walking toward home. I stopped in this diner to get a coffee and look through the classifieds again. While I was in there, I noticed that everyone was scrambling around, out of control, trying to catch up, even though there weren't that many customers. So whenever the waitress got a second I asked her why. She said the cook didn't show up, so they were all pitching in and trying to cook also. So I told her that I was a short order cook for years, and looking for work. The bossman threw me right behind the line that very minute." He kind of smiled proudly. I wanted to yell out all sorts of things about how everything is valid, but just said, "The world works in mysterious ways, always to our advantage if we keep our eyes open."

He got up for the next stop and looked down on me. "You may be a fool boy, but it takes all kinds to make this shit work."

"Yes sir." I agreed. The rest of the ride turned into a surreal moment in which everything I set eyes upon had meaning, had a place in this world. There was a wrapper of a honeybun underneath the seat in front of me. I thought about everything involved in getting that wrapper to that specific point in time, and where it was going to end up. Everything from the exact sugarcane field worker in Jamaica, to the guy pressing the plastic wraps into a box in California, to the factory worker in Ohio that made the tires for the delivery truck, to the kid who used his only quarter to buy his weekly treat, all the way to to the designer of the golf course landfill where the wrapper will eventually no longer see the light of day.

My theme of the day became connectivity. Everyone that I passed, I gave a gentle "Hi" just to let them know that I knew we were one. Of course, most just assumed I was off my rocker. When I came upon the bait shop parking lot, more than anything in the world, I wanted to explain to the dirty whore how we were connected, more than most. But as I walked toward the door, I noticed there were no pink stained cigarette butts. It would have to wait.

  The next task on Floyd's prestigious list was to cut down a large area of trees by the end of the stone wall. It seemed he wanted to clear out a path for vehicles to get through. He really had a sequence of events planned out for me. It was nice to be doing something other than just moving around branches and rocks aimlessly. Maybe this was a sign, God working through Floyd. God sent down a lightning bolt that said, 'Floyd! Build a wall, a road, and a mosaic windowed building. Start your own branch of Floydism, where everyone just loves one another and is happy.' Boy, sometimes I killed myself. I think it was the smell of pine that made me silly. Floyd had instructions on how to get into the tool shed. When I opened it up and saw all of the power tools I couldn't help but laugh. One minute he is telling his wife that I don't have all my marbles, and the next he is entrusting me with his ridiculously dangerous equipment. He probably figured I could only hurt myself way out in the middle of nowhere. I would do my best to prove him wrong, because it takes all kinds to make this shit work. One of my newest friends just told me that.

I started small with a tree about a foot wide and about twenty feet high. The chainsaw gave me power, like I could destroy so much more than myself. To tell you the truth, I'd never done this before and wasn't exactly sure how to cut it and which way the tree would fall. It was pretty damn exciting not knowing. Sometimes I wish I was naïve like this in everything. There's something about knowing that takes passion and nerve out of life.

The first tree fell remarkably slow and when it hit the ground it was as if it didn't make a sound. It reminded me of that old adage: If a tree falls in a forest with no one around, does it make a sound? Then I wondered if died out there in the forest would anyone hear me, would anyone know I was gone. Beyond the handful of people that knew or assumed I was alive, I didn't really exist. There were seven billion people who would never miss me. Maybe that's the core reason why people want to be famous, so there will be as many people as possible to miss them, to know that they were here, and then know that they were gone. It does sound like a nice feeling.

So after killing about a dozen trees, some barely missing me, and hearing them fall to the Earth's floor, I tried to conceive what it meant in my connectivity theme.

There was the sunlight aspect. I was opening up a path for the sun, killing off the dark and damp plants and insects, and creating a new life for the rest. I was killing the giants of the woods in order to create shelter and warmth for humans. The poetry of creating and destroying made me feel at least for one day that I was contributing. I left about mid-afternoon that day feeling as good as I can remember. I was a goddamn bona fide poet. Put a chainsaw in a man's hands and he thinks he's God all of a sudden.

On the bus back toward the city, many duties flooded my mind. There were so many things to do, and to tell you the truth it delighted me. That may have been the key to life, staying busy, always having something to take care of. I laughed out loud into the grimy back window. A young woman with thick eyeglasses turned to see what was so funny.

"It's okay, I just figured out life." I told her with no intention of revealing this truth. She pretended not to care, but I knew better. I could feel my stability start to crawl away from me. My stomach only held three days of bread and butter. Then another moronic revelation hit me, before I pulled out my pen and notebook. Food keeps humans stable. "Three meals a day!"

The girl turned around again. "Is that the key to life?" She said sarcastically. I don't think I deserved that.

I was almost over the edge, but still hanging on enough to realize the transformation. I hurried to a blank page to write down reminders: CHECK ON JOB. SELL CD'S. ASK FLOYD FOR JUMPER CABLES. Either that was it or my mind had made the switch. "Oh!" My hand furiously wrote out: HAPPINNESS ESSAY, THE MORON FACTORY. I exhaled.

I tried to focus on the passing landscape. There was an empty parking lot of a boarded-up grocery store. We were driving through the poorest area of the city. This neighborhood was several stops past my own, and even though I realized it I still just sat there predicting the future. The bus would eventually be near Club Virgo or Club Pluto, whatever it was called these days. My clothes were filthy and my head was getting more crooked by each city block, but it seemed just as good a time as any to see if they still needed a bartender. Maybe it wasn't too late for everyone.

The bus stopped right on the edge of downtown. It was a very familiar corner of the world. One that I preferred to stay away from, but we have to do what we have to do, said the responsible man trying to sneak into my head. I stepped into the club with my dusty sneakers. There were a few sharp dressed men talking at the bar. The club didn't open till early in the evening, so I assumed them to be part of the new crew of owners. They stopped talking. The one closest to me, holding an unlit cigar said, "You lost?"

"No, I'm here to see Big John about a job."

The man eyed a teenage kid mopping the floor by the bathrooms. He put down the mop and went back to where I knew the office was located. The structure of the bar was the same as when I had worked there before, but the mood had changed. They had attempted to put some class in the décor, but it was kind of like giving a new coat of paint to a crack pipe. It seemed to be a much more frightening place.

I was still by the front door taking in the new atmosphere. The cigar man turned to me. "Well? Have a seat brother, you making my man D nervous." They all laughed like villains together. I went up to the bar and sat a few stools down from them. I was a bit clammy as the memories of Club Virgo came back to me. It was a time when cash was overflowing inside my mattress, and conviction was empty in my cabinets. I didn't miss it or regret it at all. Regret is for people who forgot to fuck up, and missing things is for people who don't have holes to dig themselves out of.

"You look more like a doorman." The cigar man said. "How'd you get those raccoon eyes?"

"I wanted to prove to this girl with a scar over her cheek that I didn't have a choice."

He started to respond with something clever, I could see it coming, but we were interrupted. "What's up?" A deep voice bellowed out from behind me.

I turned around to see the infamous Big John. "Hey man. I'm Luke's friend. He recommended me for the bar position." I tried to keep it simple, knowing he was going to mention the old man I'd falsely sent over.

"Oh, another one. You hear that Eddie, another friend of Luke's." He had a sinister chuckle.

I feigned ignorance. "What do you mean?"

"I mean, what does Luke look like?"

"White kid, skinny, good-looking, blondish-brown hair, he's a good friend of mine."

"Do you always come to an interview looking like a motherfucking hillbilly?"

I became very self-conscious of my clothes. "I got locked out of my house while I was working in my garden." I can't understand where these lies come from. Sometimes my mouth couldn't keep up with the bizarre notions that popped into my head. My fingers traced up and down my dirty shorts. "I figured it would be as good time as any to come down since I had no where else to go at the moment."

"You were wrong, you should have went to the motherfucking YMCA and then to the motherfucking Gap." That got some laughs from the three pimp stooges.

"Do you know where the word motherfucker came from? I mean originally in the English language?" I asked them and then went into another farce. "The worst thing that could happen to a prostitute was to get pregnant because it ruins her profession and gives her another mouth to feed. A long time ago only prostitutes used to get abortions and the backwoods doctors that performed the dirty surgeries were considered the lowliest of the low. They didn't have a title for them so they called them motherfuckers, one who fucks a baby out of her mother. Motherfucker used to be a lot worse than it is now."

"Are you the one who worked here before, when it was Virgo?"

"Yes sir, that's right."

"Yeah I heard about you and your wiseass mouth. Well, it ain't the same joint. We made it high class, expensive drinks, custom service, none of that bullshit that was here before." He stopped and looked dead into my eyes. I didn't blink or turn away. "We got niggas in here now. Niggas with money. Niggas that think they got money. Niggas that want white folks serving them. How do you feel about that, hillbilly?"

I really liked this guy. "I ain't no one's fool, but I know the difference between when I clock-in to work and when I clock-out to go home."

He looked over at the three men who turned to listen with their eyes. I knew right then that they wanted me to work for them, not out of respect, but more as a test. "You have good timing, cause I just fired this other hillbilly that couldn't take my shit. Come in tomorrow, at six, in all black, nice, like you're going to the motherfucking prom."

"Alright, tomorrow." A rush of adrenaline went through my body. I jumped off the stool, shook Big John's hand, and nodded at the three men as I headed toward the door. Outside, the sun blinded me. The contrast of the dark club to the bright sky was an omen that I ignored at the time. I began to walk home, thanking God every few steps for always looking after me. "Just tell me where and I'll be there."

Big John told me I had good timing and he was right. There might not be a better human quality to have than timing. All those wonderfully talented humans that died at the age of 27 were perfectly timed to immortalize their souls before they turned into sadness. My feet almost went into a skip. Everything felt right, a new job, a date with a beautiful girl, all I needed was a little money to get some food, hold me over until the next day, make a load of tips, and take Babe my blue ox out on Friday. As I walked up Central Avenue, the passing cars went into slow motion, the birds stopped in the sky, the wind grabbed a hold of my ears, and I realized that the next day *was* Friday. I hadn't had anything to do in months, and out of the blue sky I had a million things to do in one day. There was a solution to everything, so I banged my head trying to work the conflict out. There was really only one answer; I had to take the job. The girl could wait, but then again, jobs are everywhere, it's possible that I could never get another date in my life, and besides, I could do any job with some satisfaction, it didn't work that way with women, but I needed money and employment just to entice a woman to be interested in me, that lumberjack thing would only fly with flirting... This indecision went on until I got back home. Life could have been worse. At least I had choices. I resigned to just follow through with my list and make a last minute decision. My next duty was to sell my CDs.

The box of, who knows, maybe a hundred discs sat waiting for me to take them away. I remembered that the box would turn into a pumpkin at ten o'clock, so my wits were still intact at the moment. I sat on the floor and thought about eating a burger or pizza, maybe getting some beer, all of the gateway drugs to happiness. My head rolled back and forth, getting the bug's view of the room.

There was hardly anything left in my apartment. You have to let go of everything in order to gain everything. I was almost there, ready to take in all that the universe was prepared to inject into me. My first attempt to get up was discouraged by these anchors that had grown from my back. I wasn't tired at the time, so maybe it was the floor? Maybe it was magnetized to my white blood cells? Then a wave of depression came over me and the room got darker. I could only see the outline of the walls, and could only hear a muffled voice coming from below the floor. It was as if I was becoming the room. I didn't fight it. My past had taught me to embrace the hum of mental conflict, and just let it pass through the system. The room became so dark that even the vague lines and corners couldn't be seen. I felt like I was being sent back in time, before there was even a single molecule of substance, before there was even space, just time, the beginning. I lost all power of my senses, no sight, sounds, smells, feelings, or taste. My body floated in nothingness. I wondered if I even existed at all. Maybe I disintegrated into one single brain cell that could only question its nonexistence? Even my vocabulary began to turn into symbols of words. It was the beginning, the end, the flowers, the shank, the running shoes, the religions, and all the deadbolt locks. It all made sense at the time.

When I opened my eyes there was no longer any dusty sunlight shadowing the room. I panicked, because I was no longer the beginning of time, I was a human who possibly could have fucked up again. I hurried outside and looked through Floyd's window at his clock: 8:53pm. Floyd was watching TV. He saw me, and assumed that I wanted to talk to him. He held up a finger and came out to me. "You can't just use the doorbell like a normal person? Never mind, what am I saying?" He rubbed his eyes like he'd just woken up.

"Floyd, do you have any jumper cables?"

"Sure do. You thinking about driving again?"

"Tomorrow. It seems I have a date." I told him proudly.

"Oh yeah, what loony bin did you break her out of?" He laughed for like twenty minutes. Everybody knew just how to crack themselves up.

"No, just Detroit or somewhere."

"I'll sit'em out for you. If I'm not here, just get the keys from Laura."

I hated hearing Floyd's wife's name. It made me shudder to think she had a real identity. "Thanks, I'll see you tomorrow." I went back inside to get the box of CDs while he lit up a cigarette. Floyd just shook his head when I passed by him with the load. The walk to The CD Depot was about a half an hour. In my weak condition, it would probably take an hour. My body was moving purely on a stumbling forward progression. What I did in order to keep going was find one object in sight, a rock, a crack in the sidewalk, a tree, a dead bird, or anything that seemed real, and then I'd think, just make it to that dead bird and that's it. Once I made it that far my mind would be clear and ready for the next Grand Canyon.

I literally fell into the glass door of The CD Depot. A cowbell clanked upon my grand entrance. The same clerk was busy being snobbishly bored. He looked down at me and then at his watch. I put the sagging box up on his counter.

"That was some good stuff last time." He started taking the cases out of the box.

"Yeah, I know."

"I feel bad that you had to give them away, even though you didn't have to." He snorted in amusement. "That was your choice you know?" My life was just periodic meetings with comedians. "I tell you what, I'll make it up to you. Pick out any single CD for yourself." He was really on a power trip.

"Thanks, you're a real philanthropist." I looked through the cassette tape selection.

There was a large round clock that looked as if it had come from my third grade classroom. It began to get close to 10:00 and he had only been through half the box. I watched the seconds go by. It was as if he was taking his time on purpose, opening every case, examining every booklet, and such. When it got to be three minutes of ten, I cleared my throat. "How's it going?"

"Fine."

"Just asking because it's almost ten."

He eyed the wall clock and then his own watch. "Hm? Looky there." Then he went back to the stack.

"So it doesn't matter?"

"What?"

"That it's almost ten?" My voiced cracked.

"Yes, it does matter. Might not have time."

"But I came in well of ten."

"That is true, but the safe automatically locks on the hour, nothing I can do."

I wanted to strangle him. Yes, I told myself, that's what I'll do, I'll strangle him, and take all of the fucking money! The time was winding down. "Let's work it out now. Say a hundred dollars for the whole box. There's probably over a hundred CDs in there, that's less than a dollar each."

"There are ninety-three."

"Yes, but still, it's a hell of a deal for you." My armpits were little hairy lakes.

"A hundred for the box?" He asked me while looking at the CD case of Tanuki Suit.

"Yes, a hundred even."

My third grade class was over in fifteen seconds. As I waited for the bell to ring, he thumbed out five twenty-dollar bills. It was as if he already had them waiting. I was going into berserk mode right before seeing the money. The green paper calmed me. I felt it happen right in front of my senses. Who knows how long I stood there staring at the money. What had I become? The five pieces of paper sat on the counter mocking me.

"You alright man?" The fat hippie bastard asked me with a sneer. "Been awhile since you've seen that much money?" He snorted a laugh again. I just stood there in a trance. The second hand on the clock ticked, my stomach fell silent, and there was a clicking and shuffling ruckus from my old CDs. The five bills still sat there, daring me to take them.

"You think I give a fuck about money?" I yelled and his eyes opened out of their assurance. "This has nothing to do with money!"

"Take it easy fellow, I was just poking fun at you."

"Poking fun at me? Your possessions are your smile. This!" I picked up the twenties. "This means nothing to me." There was a green lighter on top of a pack of Camel lights. I snatched it. He went for the phone. I flicked a flame underneath one of the bills. He hung up the phone. "What the fuck man, are you nuts?"

"Yes, yes I am. I am fucking nuts!" No, I actually couldn't be nuts if I realized it. It was as easy to watch the burning money as it would be to go on a spree of murders. The twenty created a strange flame with all sorts of blues, purples, oranges, yellows, and reds. I'd never seen anything like it. It was as if it was burning more than just paper. I thought of all the grit from the thousands of fingerprints. That's what was really burning.

"Dude! You have to leave. I'll call the police," He went for the phone again. "That's a federal offense by the way."

The last of the flame came up and burned my thumb. I released it and watched it float to the floor. The clerk's face, wide and full of fear, engraved inside my head. I went over to the middle aisle and randomly grabbed a CD. He owed me that. I showed it to him and then walked out. The September night air felt as if God had finally perfected one part of life. I laughed out loud and told myself the story of what had happened. "The look, ha, the look on his face! And only for twenty dollars! What a look!"

Even though I didn't tell myself where to go, my feet apparently knew exactly where to take me. Just up the road, a greasy Greek diner awaited the hungriest man in Arcane. It was called The Spoon. It had an incredibly low ceiling, maybe seven feet high. So between the cigarette smoke and the kitchen smoke, the whole diner had this layer of fog that literally put your head in the clouds. I sat down in a booth. Behind me were two rednecks and a bored looking woman puffing on a Marlborough 100. In front of me was a hunched over woman, probably in her sixties, also smoking and sipping on her coffee. Every minute or so we would catch eyes. She was worn down, tired of this life. I wondered what she saw inside me. Maybe the same, probably the same. I couldn't imagine living to be sixty. With so many people trying to stay healthy, trying to defy old age, trying to ignore death, shit, I don't know. It makes no sense, but I guess it's just a fear of the unknown, fear of getting on a train in the middle of the night and letting it take you to another world where heaters only exist in books and no one recognizes your cough.

The waitress made her way unconsciously through the table maze. She had these huge brown Central American eyes, sad and distant.

I ordered, "Steak and eggs, rare, and a Pabst."

She wrote it down. "The eggs?"

"Um, scrambled. And make it two please."

"It comes with two eggs."

"No, I mean two of everything, steak and eggs, and two beers... please." I had a habit of being elusive when there was money in my pocket.

She wrote something else that took longer than just the number two would have, maybe her memoir, maybe a sketch of the buffoon in front of her. But there were much stranger people in there than me. She didn't question my order. She was done with being intrigued by broken Scotch bottles. Boy, did I feel good. The diner was half-full, and all the people talking at the same time created this very fitting foggy murmur. The distant waitress gently placed my beers down on the table about two feet away from me. The first sips seized the walls of my stomach, made my head light, and made my blood turn cold. It tried to come back up, but I managed to hold it behind my tonsils. I took another sip. That one was smooth. The waitress was at the table behind me. The rednecks were being rude. "This food looks like shit." The guy with a motorcycle voice told his friend. If there was one thing I couldn't stand it was someone being rude to a server. The waitress seemed used to it, which made me sad. There are some things one shouldn't get used to, like following bronze rocks, or hearing some asshole complain about diner food. I told myself not to get involved. Just eat your food, drink your beer, and go home. That would be easy enough.

My food came, steaks still sizzling. I knew it was going to make me sick, but it didn't seem to stop me in any other aspect of life. A sputtering voice came from behind me, "Goddamn man, two steaks! You got an imaginary friend?" He said more toward his friend. It was a cue to laugh at his witty remark. I just ate without responding. "Hey man, you get it, you hear me?"

"Leave'em alone Roy." The girl said softly.

"Shut it! No one asked for your opinion."

But surprisingly, he did leave me alone, and I devoured the first plate of food. The second plate was just another whim that seemed right at the time. I finished one of the beers and then slid over the second steak. The waitress dropped the check with the rednecks.

"Watch this," The bigger of the two idiots told the other. "Hey Maria, if you think I'm paying for this shit then you're fucking es-tu-pido."

I sort of turned to check out what was happening. She stormed back to the table, but spoke calmly. "You ate it, and you're paying for it."

"Shit, I'll puke it back up on the plate if that's all you want."

"Goddammit Roy!" His girl blurted out, but stopped short.

"What did I tell you?"

The waitress walked away again. I knew that getting involved would only worsen the situation, but they were ruining the first real meal I had eaten in weeks.

"It seems you have lost your dream." I told the two men. It was meant to confuse them, and it served the purpose.

"What? Lost my what?"

"I haven't known you long, but I can tell that you have lost your dream, and you've become so desperate to find it that you are looking in the most outrageous places, for instance, you're digging in between a stranger's pride." I said in the direction of the waitress. She stood two tables over. There were other assholes to take care of.

"Shut your mouth freak, come back to planet Earth." The quiet one told me in a way that was all childhood catch-up. I felt bad for him.

"What if that waitress was your mom, would you want some asshole talking to her like that?"

"You calling my mom a Mexican?" Poor guy just couldn't think for himself.

"Last chance son." Roy threatened me.

Now, I know for a fact that most adults are cowards and will avoid physical confrontation at any cost, but the great thing about rednecks is that usually they have managed to keep a junior high mentality way up into their thirties and forties, until they just get too tired. Just like a fourteen year old, they have nothing to lose and they don't understand algebra yet.

I barked like a German Shepard would.

"Let's beat the shit out of this fucker," The quieter one almost whispered, which was a verified sign that conflict was probably going to happen.

"Let's just go, no fighting tonight." The girl pleaded, and Roy went back to scolding her, happy to have someone he could control. I went back to eating my steak and beer. In between bites I let out soft barks, just because I liked the way it sounded. The rednecks were dangerously quiet. As I took a sip and looked across to the next booth, the old woman's eyes had changed. They were no longer giving up, they changed into warning signs. Her finger pointed behind me, and I felt a sharp crash into my skull.

After that, what happened, well, I don't know, but I do remember little things. First there was a gush of some red liquid all over my head, face, and hands. The room was a solid picture of people staring below the fog. Then there were hands grabbing me and leading me outside. There were flashing lights and sirens. Time ran backwards. The smell of adhesive clicked in mists. The hands made me lay down and I was put into a bright room. There were all these blurry shadows and voices. Then a vivid moment came and it woke me from the confusion. The red liquid was on my lips. My tongue swiped over the liquid. It was ketchup. As soon as the taste recognition kicked in, all of my other senses suddenly came back. My eyes could see the inside of an ambulance and a paramedic staring at me. My ears could make out the siren clearly. The ends of my nerves felt my body lying on a stretcher. "Where are you taking me?" I asked the lady above me.

"We're taking you to the hospital." She didn't pluck her eyebrows. I liked that.

"Why did you come, I think I'm fine, I'm fine."

"You probably have a concussion, and you're going to need stitches."

"Did I get hit with a ketchup bottle?"

"I believe so."

"That makes sense." I concluded.

"What makes sense?"

"They should switch to those plastic bottles, it's easier to get the ketchup out."

She laughed. "Yes, that would make sense."

That wasn't what I meant, and for some reason I thought she would understand, but little rectangular pieces of flesh got in the way of my explaining. "Do I get charged for this?" I believed insurance existed solely in the next breath.

"Don't worry, you can take care of that later. Right now your health is most important." She said, like she was reading a manual.

"I don't care about my health." I said calmly, and almost as a question. "I do care about how much the ambulance costs."

"You have insurance right?" She must have been crossing her fingers.

"No, and I'm broke."

"Well the hospital will work it out. Just sit back and we'll take care of you."

Any decent American company knew exactly how to *not* answer your questions. "I want to refuse service. I didn't call you, so I want out now." The ambulance seemed to already be parked, so it was as good time as any to refuse service. The back doors opened. We were already at the emergency room entrance. It hit me that the hospital was only like two or three blocks away from the diner. "I could have walked here!" A man in white stood outside the ambulance with a wheelchair. He came toward me to help me out. "I can walk, thanks."

"That's fine, but it's hospital regulations. You have to be wheeled in, no choice." He said.

"I'm not going in, so that takes care of that." I hopped out and started walking away from the emergency room. I had a paranoid thought that they actually brought me to the mental hospital. It would make more sense than a medical hospital.

"Sir? Sir!" My lady came after me. "I highly recommend you come back. You could have permanent neurological damage." If she only knew the truth. I kept going. "You could go into a coma. Sir?" She yelled back at someone to get an officer.

"Thank you for your help." I didn't look back.

"Don't go to sleep." She yelled. What a nice lady. I kind of felt bad, but there was nothing to do. I would rather have just gone into a coma right there in the diner. It would have been the perfect time to fade away. I had money in my pocket, a full meal and beer in my stomach, a job, a date, and an ending act of chivalry to boot. It would have been a perfect moment to die, but I guess even I don't have that great of timing.

My lady paramedic friend was right though, I couldn't go to sleep. I didn't want to commit suicide directly, just a little poisoning at a time. The old train station became my destination. That would kill a few hours. The air above the tracks smelled like polluted bandages, tomatoes, sugar, and diesel fuel. There was a stoic freight train parked at the spot where only ghosts were supposed to be. The hobo told me it had been ten years since the last train had come through. This must have been part of that train. I crawled up into an empty boxcar and sat on the edge where a light shone down. I took out my notebook and began concentrating on the thin blue lines on the page. They were like veins ready to explode. There were still some remnants of glass and congealed red gook in my hair. I wasn't sure if it was pieces of my skull and blood. My fingers traced over the cut on a lump. Between the page and the open wound I couldn't help but wonder if there was any difference at all between medicine, locomotives, guts, and a choice of notes. She was confusing; life, survival, emotions, fate, I didn't know what was real. She wanted to be shocked, she didn't want to let us down, life, survival, emotions, fate. I waited for her to tell me when she was ready. The page says it all, but the wound would remain open.

I started writing about how happiness is red, and it tells lies, I think... It was a bunch of words, unconnected, unstable, unreadable, yet solid forms of letters filling page after page. The light shining down on my hand had a subtle tinkering about it that dictated the mood. My heart was beating like it was on it's way out, gasping for one last thump, out of control, a maniac at the wheel, and blaming what was above. I stopped writing, started sobbing. I thought the fever was gone, thought that food and a good knock over the head had cured me, but it was stronger than ever. A fog drifted into the train yard. It was thin, and quite apparent that it was for me. My hands pressed against the boxcar floor as if they were trying to become a part of the steel structure. I lifted them up and stared at the soot-like dirt that hid my fingerprints. The black covering intrigued me to no end. It reminded me of this Native American tribe that would cover the palms of their human sacrifice, and right before burning the body alive they would clean the person's hands. In effect, it was to uncover the numbness and it let them reach out to their spirit God or spirit horse or spirit cactus or something.

I hopped down off the train and began walking the tracks back toward home. Lingering ground clouds dampened my clothes and face. I still fought with the decision of work or woman. I hadn't had a difficult decision such as this in years. I did have money... Then it hit me. The diner! My dirty hand pulled out four twenty-dollar bills from my pocket. I didn't pay the waitress.

"First thing in the morning, I will go down there, yes, first thing." The scene would be quite dramatic. I couldn't wait for them to see the admirable and indestructible guest of the year. There would be talk of this hero for years. He came in and ordered not one, but two steaks, not one, but two beers at once, then he defends the poor immigrant waitress trying to put her kids through school, just trying to put food on the table, then he was blindsided, yes that's right, struck from behind, it is true, and then he was carted off, thought to be dead. What happened then? The hero walks back in the next day, not only to pay his bill, but to leave the damsel a magnificent tip. Yes, it would be an amazing morning for the downtrodden. I was going to make sure of that.

The tracks hit a long straight line. As the rising sun painted the sky purple, I could just barely see the point of the tracks meeting the horizon. That was where I needed to go, to that horizon. If I made it there, the women and jobs wouldn't matter. The decision would be made tomorrow. Whatever and wherever God led me would be my answer, and then and only then would I pick up the paintbrush again.

i named it breathing...

Day 12,307

It could have been a week later, an hour later, maybe a year. My paramedic friend's words, "Don't fall asleep." echoed in my head. It was exciting, like time travel. Maybe doctors froze my brain for a society control study? Maybe my whole life was a scientific experiment? My thoughts went outside my body and I could see an image of my body locked down on a blinding white bed. My skull was open like shutters in an old haunted house. There were scientists playing piano keys on my brain. A-minor made me burn money, E-flat forced me to eat dead people's flowers, the 5th Symphony cut all strings of rationalism and fear... I opened my eyes and it was just my plain old apartment. At least it wasn't a mental hospital. I mean, I guess it wasn't. I know it was daytime. The cut on my head was swollen and crusty, nothing that a hat couldn't take care of. It seemed like only hours had gone by. I sort of wished that a whole day had passed so I wouldn't have to make a decision between work or girl. It was raining outside. I only had on boxers, so I put on sandals and went out to look at Floyd's clock. Thank God Floyd's wife wasn't in their living room. It was 12:48pm. I still needed to go back to the diner and pay the waitress, but it would have to be after the rain. It was coming down in buckets.

It seemed as good an opportunity as any to go out to check on my tomatoes. I stared out at the sheet of water coming down. My boxers were still wet from checking the time. The storm was one of those heat exhaustions where the sky just couldn't take the constant buildup of humidity and carbon monoxide. God was cleansing the sky above me, hoping for once I would see clearly. I walked slowly to the backyard, treating it like a cold shower. The yard had formed a thin pool over the grass. I patted down the soil in the garden. The heavy spurt of rain wasn't good after such a dry spell. The dirt wouldn't know how to handle it. I wiped my muddy hands over my body as if it were soap. The cut on my head became raw and soft. I figured that the rain had to be good for it. The sky boomed and lightning struck down in the distant trees. I became unnerved, impatient, thinking God was going to make me a part of the storm, a vibration in the cycle of nature. As the rain came down even harder and the wind pushed through the drops more precisely, I became more obsessive. I tried running with wind, but the direction was unstable, yes, the direction was unstable. It started to make sense. I became mad with conclusion, with indecision, with spontaneity. I ran over to my tomato plants and ripped one of the greenish balls off the vine and sunk my teeth into the flesh. It was tough and sour, but I swallowed it anyway, then took another bite, then another, it made my skin crawl, it made my jaw lock up, but I kept going, kept going until my stomach muscles clinched together, and the pieces of skin and seed came rushing back up my throat and back to the Earth. The rain curled around my ears, my hair poured around my neck, and washed off the acidic saliva. I got it all out and then went into a series of dry heaves. God's water now seemed warm, almost hot, almost scorching hot. It formed a waterfall down my nose. With my mouth open toward the sky, I went back inside and found the only towel. I needed a woman. I needed someone to save me. My mind was made up. A job couldn't save me, only kill me. A woman would kill me a little at a time while inspiring me to do normal things and think like an idiot. I would never go back to Club Pluto. It would defeat me like in all the myths.

    The CD case that I randomly picked from The Depot was on the floor beside my shirt. Music had to save me, not a woman. Fuck women! Fuck jobs! Only music could fuck me right! I opened it and there wasn't a CD inside, just the liner notes. It was a sign from the devil. It was perfect! I took them out, reading the words out loud. "I dropped a double brandy and tried to recall the events..." Ah Mr. Dylan, I surpassed you many years ago, and decided to be drunk all the time, drunk on life, on absurdness, on your music, on everything that floats in the cracks of wood floors. "...bought a serpent from a passing angel - yeah the good old days are gone forever and the new ones aren't far behind..." I read on, in awe, in love, in love with those fucking people who love eternity. Goddamn those people! I was so excited about life all of a sudden. I was in need to find that one fucking heart out there that beat in deafening waves of bass drum bliss. I would piss off a million dead souls to find it.

    I put on my swim trunks, my sandals, one of my three shirts, and that Yankees baseball cap. The waitress probably wouldn't even recognize me without ketchup running down my head. The rain had slowed, but within twenty seconds I was soaked. The walk was incredible. Life was incredible. I felt as if I was going to die at any moment. A car hit a puddle and sprayed the dirty road water up on me. If only that would have happened the day before, everything would be so much different. It reminded me of when I was being baptized as a kid, and how my dad the pastor dunked me under the dirty water. I got the bizarre notion to fill my lungs with water also. It made sense. I took a bath every day, but when did I ever drown, and since I was being *born again* the only thing to do was literally test the waters. I grabbed a hold of my dad's hand and leaned back with all my weight. He was bigger than me, so he eventually pulled me up. Some of the Deacons came running up, and they pretended to revive me, but I was just out of breath, not dead. Ever since then, being reborn has always obsessed me.

I walked into The Spoon diner dripping wet. I shook like a dog on the red carpet. The fog sat under the ceiling even damper than usual. The smell of bacon made my stomach rumble.

"Sit anywhere." A waitress told me from across the room. So I went back to the same booth as the night before, looking around for any loose skin or part of an opinion. The waitress approached the table with a wet rag and a menu. "How is it out there?"

"It's just like in here, only we're in here." I had a habit of never answering a small-talk question normally. She just wiped the table and made it a part of the blinking of eyes. I was pretty soaked, but the booth was warm. "I was the one who got hit with the ketchup bottle last night."

She looked at me like an abstract painting. I think she thought that I was coming to get something for free. "Are you alright?"

I didn't know how to answer that question. "I didn't pay my check, because, I don't know, I guess I had a concussion or something."

"But you're alright now?"

"Dandy, thank you for asking, just a slight cut, a few stitches, that's all, well, thirteen stitches in all, but I feel wonderful, thank you for asking." I thought since she was pretending to care about my health, I should at least return the favor. "But I would like to take care of my check. It was two orders of steak and eggs, and a couple of beers."

"Okay, I'll check on it. Would you like anything to drink?"

"Just a side of bacon please."

As I sat there, the voices from around the restaurant mingled into a ball of paranoia. I began talking to myself out loud, unaware that I was out in public. "A riot? What! That is absurd. Just calm down, there's nothing here that can hurt you, by God, you took a great blow to your head, but someone will save you, something in this world will put an end to this. Ah, so sure they will come through." I paused, for all of a sudden I heard a passing train. I looked around at the other people. Some hid their eyes from me.

They didn't want to admit that there was a train coming through the doors. "Do you hear it?" I asked anyone listening. "It's not a lie, I know that for sure. It's a goddamn locomotive!"

The waitress startled me with the plate of bacon. It was disgusting looking, curled up pieces of brown pig fat over a pool of grease. "Your check was taken care of." She said.

"What's this?" I pushed the plate away.

"A side of bacon." She felt trouble. "That's what you ordered."

"Did I? Well, there's nothing to do about it then."

"Anything else?"

I'm not sure if I said anything, or if my expression said it all, but she just placed the check down and left quickly. I tried to ask her before she got away. "Is there a train track behind the building?" But she was gone. The bill was $1.50. "A dollar fifty for this swine. What is this world coming to? Pigs made of gold, trains with ghosts of slaughterhouses." I took my napkin and wrapped it around the three bacon slabs, put a twenty on the table, and went back out into the rain.

About halfway home the sun came out while the rain still wet the streets. The napkin stuck to the limp bacon. I peeled off the paper as best as possible and stuffed the mixture in my mouth, chewing with delight while walking with purpose. I loved this city so much. It seemed as if destroying it would be the only way to really show it the proper affection. These thoughts of destruction reminded me of my meeting that was supposed to take place at eight that night. One of the dozens of banks on the way home boasted an electronic clock that read 5:13pm and then 84 F. Weird. Numbers. Time. I wanted to see the symbols and not understand. It enraged me to be a part of someone else in the world that just read the exact same time. The rain stopped. I felt like a murderer with all that fat stuck in between my teeth. It was a good feeling. I sucked at the last pieces. My mind was loose and it was confusing to me, because it had been days since, wait, what was the day, was it Friday? Had I yet to figure this out? This is what a good meal of fried pig does to you. The brain only needs contradictions to work properly.

My front door held a new comfort that I'd never felt before. I picked up the phone and started to punch in Luke's number. Obviously the phone didn't work. I needed to apologize for not showing up for my first day on the job. I really liked that Big John character too. He was the kind of boss that would abuse the shit out of you on the job and then hug you afterward. I just knew this about Big John. Then I sighed, and I only mention it, because I never sigh, maybe once a year. It was the wall. It looked down on me. I began stripping the wet clothes off my body and looking for the one brick in the wall that would soothe me. It was full of my hero's words and some of my own little moments of clarity.

"A penetrating intelligence anticipates this by watchfulness." Unknown.

"Is man merely a mistake of God's? Or is God merely a mistake of man's." Nietzsche.

"Yes, I'm stupid, but so is the moon." Bukowski.

"Sometimes I could see her, but I could never reach far enough." Alex.

"All my lies are just wishes." Tweedy.

"Cheetos can make your dick turn orange." This was one of my own brilliant assumptions of life.

It made me laugh out loud. Then I read it again and began laughing hysterically. "It's true! Yes! It does make your dick turn orange!" I jumped up and went to take a real shower. There was still a little soapy residue. It's amazing what a man can get by with in such a clean society. This ritual was only for my own peace of mind. Dirt-riddled buffoons would lead the revolution. I know that for a fact. Men wearing cologne don't want to be men, despite what the commercials tell us.

When I knocked on Floyd's door, his wife answered. "You must want those jumping cables." She told me as if she knew my secret.

"Yes, the *jumper* cables are at the top of my want list."

"I'll get the car!" She then closed the door in my face. I went over to Charlie and leaned back on the freshly rinsed hood. The sky held tiny white puffs like babies. Floyd's wife pulled her blue sedan through the yard and popped the hood. She was a regular auto genius. You could tell that she had seen the process about a million times, but had never actually gotten a chance to do it herself. She took the cables and went to work, almost pushing me out of the way. "Get out of the way." She ordered me. She went to start up her car and gave me a weird pit crew thumbs-up. I turned the ignition and a sound of harsh static came and went. I knew it, I knew God would curse me for making the wrong decision... again, as he should. "Just turn an eye for once goddammit!"

"What?" Floyd's wife thought I was talking to her.

"I said, not yet."

She pushed down on the gas, revving up the engine. "Try again." Another thumbs up.

"Fuck you God!" I said and turned the switch at the same time. It started. Which just meant that I would be crippled in a horrible car accident later. I gave her a double thumbs-up back. She was deliriously happy. Boy, the kicks it takes to excite her! I wish I could just sit back and piss on myself because a car started. She was so excited in fact that she almost fried herself. Floyd's wife took off one end of the jumper cable clamps and accidentally touched metal to metal. An electric crack sounded and sparks ensued. She skipped around the yard while thinking of heaven. I grabbed the rubber linings and held them apart. "It's fine, I think." She had an expression of death and I smiled at her how I imagine an angel would look down upon someone uselessly. It made my day to know that Laura could think about dying. It made me think of her as a real person with a real name.

I let Charlie run while I got ready for whatever awaited me. I would have asked Laura what day it was but the anticipation excited me, like starting a car or something. I picked out a few mixed cassette tapes, some conversation starters. Before taking off, I ran over to Floyd's window where Laura was back to ignoring life. I banged on the glass, scaring the hell out of her. She looked into my eyes, and I yelled, "God bless you Laura, you're a saint, a real live angel!"

She didn't respond. She turned her head as if I was a maniac for complementing her. I backed Charlie out into the clean street. It felt pretty strange to be driving again.

There were dead bugs on my windshield. The rain couldn't take them off. I put the first mix tape in, and my blown speakers blasted out *Sympathy for the Devil*. We hit Central Avenue with all of its potholes and lumps and construction and character of how Arcane used to be before it needed to be aesthetically nice to survive. Charlie embraced the character and I sang with the windows down. When the song was done I rewound it and sang it again. Then I did it again, over and over until reaching the bait shop. Babe the blue ox was waiting out in the parking lot, smoking a cigarette, seemingly unconcerned. I guess I was late, but at least it was Friday. She came up to Charlie and stuck her head in the window. "Right on time, I'm impressed."

"That's me... punctual."

She got in with her cigarette. "Mind if I smoke?" I forgot how sexy and raspy her voice was.

"Take a look around. I think there's asbestos growing in the ceiling. Smoke couldn't do much else to it."

She looked up and around in agreement. "So where are we going? You're not taking me to the woods to kill me, are you?"

"Not yet, but we'll see how the night goes." I had forgotten what it was like to try and be witty and fake and all that shit that gets one laid.

"I want to get drunk, like so drunk I won't be able to think of my name." She tossed her butt out the window.

"What is your name by the way?"

"Luna. Yours?"

"Luna? Interesting. People have so many names for me, so it isn't important."

"Oh, we're playing that game."

I smiled and rubbed the hair on my chin.

"Where are we going?" She asked again.

"I don't know, driving until we stop sort of thing."

"You're the tour guide. I've seen enough trees and lakes for seven lifetimes, so stay away from those."

"So why did you move?"

"I thought we had covered this?"

"Yes," I rubbed my chin again. Where did this come from all of a sudden? Maybe I always did it, but only noticed it around Luna. God, how old was she? Probably twenty-one, twenty-two? I made the right decision. There wouldn't be many times left in my life in which I could go out with youth. "We did cover it in a polite way, in a way in which you avoided the details and the truth."

"There was a line of very important worm customers."

"Wormers."

"Yeah, wormers, and you don't get to know why I'm really here, yet."

"Everything begins with lucid indifference." I brought out the Camus right away, before Miller, Nietzsche, and even Yeats. Yeats was a finisher though. Camus was a starter.

"Oh yeah?" She was skeptical. She stared out her window. "Are you going to teach me about life to get me in bed?"

I smiled guiltily. "That would be ideal, but I'm more of a realist. I planned on spitting out intelligent-sounding quotes at you all night while feeding you multiple alcoholic beverages, just in hopes that you'd kiss me to shut me up."

"That's realistic to you?"

"You don't want to know what reality is to me. That was just a fantasy of a normal dysfunctional date."

"We're on a date?" She was really busting my balls.

I thought about it for a couple of seconds. "Yes, we are on a date. Hey, here's where I used to teach." We passed by East High School.

"You look like a teacher, like a gym teacher that has to teach one real class so he chooses philosophy or sex-education."

"Dead on." My eyes averted down toward her white Elvis boots.

"Watch the road, buddy."

"And up here are more trees, and then a little further up is one of our many precious strip malls. We pride ourselves in the labyrinthine parking lot designs in which there are many ways in, but only one way out."

"Wow, tell me more."

I reached down to turn up the stereo. I wanted to see if she reacted to the song. She didn't. "And in a few minutes we'll be embarking on a variety of bars that boast hot wings, TV sports, and men that give high-fives and talk about their lawn mowers."

"No other choices?"

"A few, but this will be much better for us to make fun of. Plus these bars are the epitome of the city, and that's the point, tonight, for a little while at least."

We drove through the downtown area pointing and making condescending sounds of impression. The first bar delivered just what I promised. It was one of the many brand new restaurants that attempted to look old and rustic like a barn. We sat at a corner table that was on a raised section overlooking the rest of the space. There was a gaggle of businessmen spread out around the large oval shaped bar. We didn't talk at first. There were too many distractions. It was lazy and depressing. She must have been thinking the same. "Do you think this is sad?"

"This?" I pointed at me and then at her.

"No, all this." She wafted her hand around like a game show host.

"I think if you look at any aspect of life hard enough then you'll find it sad."

The waitress approached us with menus. It was sad. We ordered beers. It was sad. She opened the menu. It was sad. I had sixty dollars. It was sad. I became nervous. It was sad. "I mean we're humans... we're tragic in every aspect, because there's too much to analyze."

"I think this is sad," She said. "I think I'm sad, but, I don't know, but..."

"But you're fine. We're all temporarily fine, we're all temporarily not fine. It's not supposed to be fluent." I paused to let her interject, but she didn't seem to need to. "Man seeks his own misery by creating false icons and these distractions of happiness." I needed to interject with a quote from my essay.

"But doesn't less distractions create more time for thinking about life and miseries?" She took a slug off her beer as soon as the waitress put it down. "Why are we talking about this?"

"You brought it up."

"Yeah, but I just wanted you to agree with me and then we could go back to silently judging."

The waitress was still behind us. "May I get you anything to eat right now?"

My stomach clinched up. "I'm fine." I knew if I didn't order then she wouldn't either.

"I'm starving, let's get some nachos." She didn't look up from the menu, and before I could say anything the waitress walked away.

"I guess I could eat something, it's... just, such a huge lunch." I put my hand over my belly.

"Oh yeah, what did you have?"

What a rude question! Who would want to know such things? "Bacon."

She laughed. "You're weird, but a funny weird."

"Give me a few hours, I'll have you on the floor with my weirdness."

She laughed again. It had been so long since a woman had laughed at me, or at least with me. Plenty of women have laughed at me, I'm sure.

"Who creates false icons?" She asked.

"Are you kidding?"

"No. I mean, what makes them false?"

"It's all false. Look at those men stare up into the television. They worship it. They don't want to see anything real. They're afraid to even look at their own shit.

It helps them get through the fiscal year. It's just like you said, it's sad."

"What about you? How are you sad?"

I became silent. "I'm sure the list is long and prestigious, but as a personal goal, I try not to think about the past too much. Maybe that's what's sad about me, but I don't think so, it makes me light, free, and that's not sad. How about you?"

"No, no, the question is still on you."

She watched the wheels turning in my head.

"I tell you what," She said. "If you are completely honest with me, I'll do the same."

"This is a trick. You see the difference between you and I, is that you *want* to tell me your tragedy."

"No I don't. I just thought it would be neat to actually be honest on a first... encounter." She caught herself from saying the word *date*.

The word *honest* rang through my head. I couldn't figure out what that was. We all are lying constantly. When we are honest, we are just being honest about a role we played in the past, acting, conceptualizing our own paths. "I can't understand certain things in life. It's like numbers. Like the word happy, whenever I try to picture it, it comes out backwards or jumbled or in the form of an animal or something, sometimes in the form of everything, but either way I wake up with bruises, and headaches, and I'm starving and friends are gone, and I forget to participate in life, and sometimes I forget to wake up at all..." I took a sip of beer while looking up at the TV. "But I'm not sad, I'm never sad. I never look in the mirror, I never forget to dream, and I never understand what's going on, and maybe that's my tragedy? Understanding. But the more I don't understand, the more I learn and become addicted to the process, it's like picking at a scab until it becomes a scar. I know there's going to be a scar, even though it doesn't have to be that way."

She kept her bottle in front of her lips without drinking. "I moved down here because I needed help. I have bulimia. That's my secret." She looked up toward the TV's.

"Yes! That's what I have also! Except different... I have this insatiable appetite for life, but I purposely throw it all back up." I was so happy. "There needs to be a word for it, a name."

"God I'm starving." She smiled. We caught eyes and began laughing, me without any noise. I wondered if she thought I was being condescending about her disease. And to be honest, before this conversation I thought that bulimia and anorexia were both just mentally deficient American diseases in which the victim got what they deserved, but whenever I related it to my own unnamed disease, it made sense. The nachos came and we ordered two more beers. I thought about telling her that I only had sixty dollars, but sometimes honesty had its limits. I could tell her every single detail about how psycho I was, but could never admit to being broke. We devoured the whole plate, all the way down to the last bit of hardened cheese. She got up to go to the bathroom and looked down at me. "Wish me luck." She showed me her crossed fingers.

"Oh, who cares, puke it up." I may not have been the best date for Luna.

After she left I tried to give my disease a name. My eyes scanned the room looking for ideas. It was getting crowded with loosened ties and condensed dreams. This was the beginning of a two-day bender, a disease that made one forget that Monday morning was inevitable for the rest of their lives. If one was lucky, Monday turned into a fishing pole and a nurse wiping your chin, if one was lucky. The waitress began clearing the table. "Yaw doing good?"

"Yes, thank you." It took about an eighth of a second for me to go from polite customer to a repeat stage actor offender. "Do you have champagne here?"

"I'm not sure, maybe?" She was chewing cinnamon gum.

"It's our anniversary, seven years. We met right outside this building, by the tracks, back before the place was a bar. The short version is, well, I won't bore you, but let's just say, she saved my life." The waitress wanted to leave. "Anyway, I just thought it would be nice to celebrate with some bubbles, you know how festive it is, but don't worry about it, just forget I asked. I thought it would be nice, that's all, but don't worry about it, beer is our favorite anyway."

"No, I'll check." She held the dishes uncomfortably.

"Please don't, I was just wondering, besides, I'm driving, I shouldn't."

She needed to get away from the babbling fool. Luna came walking back up. She had an amazing body, bulimia or not. It was a real woman's body, all curves, perfect legs, hips, and butt, all full and tight. I thought about being inside her and the timing was off, because she slipped into my mind. "What were you just thinking about?"

"Nothing." God I was a moron!

"We're supposed to be honest, remember?"

"Did you throw up?"

"Maybe. What were you thinking about?"

"Your hips."

"My hips?"

"Yeah, I was imagining holding them." I smiled with a cocky embarrassment. "See what you get when you're honest. An honest man is just a perverted man in our world."

"You want to hold my hips?"

I couldn't tell if that was an invitation or another verifying question. Before I could figure it out, the waitress came up with two glasses of champagne. "Happy anniversary!" She was so proud of herself for coming through. I didn't care if it was a lie, I was just wondering if she was going to make me pay for them. Luna gave me a suspicious head tilt. Then she leaned over the table and kissed me. "Happy anniversary."

I knew right then I was dealing with a crazy woman. "By the way, I've never had bulimia."

"By the way, I only have sixty dollars."

The next bar was a dark hole in the wall on the outskirts of the skyscrapers. When Double Room wasn't hosting live blues, you could get cheap beers. I had been banned from there, but that was at least a couple hundred days before, and unlike people, bars tend to forgive and forget. Plus, it was just busy enough for me to blend in. I imagined that without my crazy eyes people couldn't recognize me. She sat across from me, no smile, her legs weren't crossed, and I'm pretty sure there were at least three men gawking at her. The bar wasn't known for its flock of women. I extended my hand over our beers and at first offered, but realizing she'd never take it, I snagged the ends of her fingers and pulled her over to me with nothing better to say except, "If they only would have made you perfect." Then I thought of days when it rained ice, nights when the road was as black as the sky, and the way that circles were just as imperfect as the Earth. But she didn't let go, because it was new. Every woman is a genius of the normal man, but ever since I was told that my parents were false and that Santa Claus was real at the same time, it only made sense that I would say abnormal things.

"So are you going to offer information about your black eyes, or do I have to just come out and ask it?"

"Oh this? This is just something I got over in England."

"I don't think I like you." She tried to get caught in a lie.

"What do you think is wrong with you?" I felt arrogant, powerful, and slightly God-like. I might not have ever written a decent poem in my life, but goddamn if there wasn't always poetry around me.

She couldn't answer. Why was sex or heartache always the final answer? Guilt and actor's shoes were always the score? "I have to tell you that I'm a Christian, not like a bible-thumper but I go to God for answers."

"And if God doesn't give you answers?" I asked.

"He always does, in different forms."

"Why do you feel like you have to tell me that?" I had a habit of setting questions up in order to get my own words out.

"Because most of my friends thought I was stupid for being religious, for believing in God, and I thought we'd attempt to keep on this honesty route."

"So what is God telling you now?"

"See, that's the cynicism I expected." She lit a cigarette.

"No, not at all, I believe in God also, it's just a different one than most."

"Different, like how?"

"Different just like you and I are different. I believe I am my God, I believe you are your God, like in the way that there is always a voice in our heads telling us what to do and what not to do. It goes along with our duty to our self. When we stop listening to our God, then it's the same as sin, same as blasphemy."

"I don't agree with that, because there are some fucked up things in my head that I couldn't obey."

"But that's not your God talking, that's the world's influence. Your God is what stopped you from the continuation of the influence."

"Can you really decipher the difference? If it's in your head, and you believe God is your thoughts then I just can't separate the two." She looked at the ashtray as if her God was telling her to put out the cigarette.

"I'm not saying you have to buy into it, it's just my thing."

She smiled. "Did you ever think of a name for your disease?"

I thought about it for a few seconds. "Yeah… I named it breathing."

Later that night as she cuddled her naked body up to me, I looked her over and thought about how sad she must be to be there with me. She passed out and I stared past her head into the wall. When I would wake up in the morning, there would just be another bruise. But at that moment it was nice to get punched. It made words clearer, and put letters in the correct order.

Part 3

god is that brief moment in time in which everything makes sense...

Day 12,308

The night went by with me staring at the ceiling and walls, but mostly the ceiling. I could smell Luna all over the room. How could any man sleep with such a heavenly cloud of woman in the air? That smell could make a man do amazing things, like get a job, buy furniture, kill another human, join a cult, cheat on a wife, cuddle like a liar, laugh at a mother, set oneself on fire, renounce God, or at the very worst it could give a man hope. It's no coincidence that there's so much fatality in sex. Its purpose is to create, and its side effects to destroy. The curtains became brighter and she woke. I expected her to be paranoid and shameful, just wanting to get back alone, or back beside a toilet. She grabbed my wrist and pulled me in closer, putting my fingers over her perfectly small breasts. I had to admit to being a bit taken back. Unsure of how to relax, I looked for anything comfortable. There was a notebook on the floor, the one with my unfinished essay. The open page had all of my crossed-out ideas and titles. It might as well have been my guardian angel's daily log of my life.

"Do you have any sisters or brothers?" She whispered.

"I have a little sister. She's my whole life."

"Good, I don't trust people that don't have siblings."

"How many do you have?" I said into her hair. It smelled like peaches and smoke.

"None," She held her breath. "So are you really a lumberjack or what?"

I didn't answer at first. This is the point in which we separate ourselves, that is, bums and women.

"Or what?" She guessed.

"What, you know, or what."

"Oh, one of those guys. Sleep with him on the first night, and he shrinks up into a mysterious alien that can only answer yes or no questions."

"It's not that. That's the easy part, saying things. People say things that they don't mean all the time, but they keep on talking. It's the reason we initiate sex, it's one of the only real things that we do. That awkward pause of conversation is a force of nature, people just get tired of bullshitting at the same time." I said.

"You do a great job of avoiding questions, very elaborate."

I still didn't answer.

She flipped over really quickly. "Are you a criminal?"

"Yes."

"Are you a murderer?"

"No, yes."

"Are you a thief?"

"Definitely."

"What do you steal?"

"The things they don't put you in jail for, comfort, pride, superficiality, shit. I don't know."

"That's too bad. I hoped you stole cars, jewelry, or robbed banks."

"Yeah, I wish I did also." That's when the idea popped in my head. Why not? Why not steal things they could throw you in jail for? Three meals a day, structure, recreation, I could start smoking, and I could actually write everyday without the hassle of the outside world telling me what to do. Maybe get a solid twenty-year sentence. It would be the equivalent of the time warp I'm always wishing for. I could really put myself in an uncomfortable position, really know what it's like to suffer with chains.

"What are you thinking of?" She asked in a voice that surpassed all of the qualities that a woman will sooner or later unleash upon you. In short, she all of a sudden sounded sweet.

"Steal a little and they throw you in jail, steal a lot and they make you king."

"Huh?"

"Dylan, he stole a lot, so they made him a king."

"What did he steal?"

"He stole a lot of pride, but he had a microphone and radio towers..." Maybe that's what I needed, a microphone, no, never mind, that would be disastrous.

"You're pretty strange." She turned over and put her feet to the floor as if she was leaving.

"The fatality of sex." I said forgetting these were my thoughts and not hers.

"What does that mean?"

"Nothing, something I was concluding to myself earlier. How sex is fatal, final. There's nowhere to go after sex, except to sleep, or church, or a confused place inside oneself."

"Those *are* places. Anyway, I have to go home." She put on her jeans. I stared at every disappearing inch of skin as the denim covered it. "You don't have anything… I mean, you don't have chairs or shoes or stuff." She snapped her bra back on. I was heartbroken. "Are you really broke or were you kidding about that being your last sixty dollars?"

My mind flashed back to the last bar we went to. I pulled out my last five dollars and bought us one beer to share, leaving the bartender a dollar-fifty tip. "Yeah, broke."

"Well, take me home, and you can go out and make some more money. You can't expect me to fuck you without getting me drunk first." She was my kind of Christian.

I looked up at her, clothed and not smiling. "I guess that does make it easier, a system."

I drove her back toward the bait shop. We were mostly silent until she brought up a forgotten memory. "You yelled at me last night. You never said you were sorry."

"Really, I don't remember yelling." I truly didn't.

"I was trying to open that bottle of champagne in your refrigerator, and you freaked out."

"Oh... yeah, you didn't know, it's just a cheap bottle of wine, but, it means something."

"You waiting for a celebration?"

I laughed. "No, it has nothing to do with that."

"What does it have to do with?"

"I'm sorry I yelled at you. I never yell."

We didn't talk about it anymore. I was avoiding the question and she knew it. As a matter of fact, we didn't talk at all until we got to the bait shop. She pointed out her truck. As Charlie hit the gravel parking lot, a devastating view crept into my sight. It was the other older cashier outside holding a cigarette. Luna responded first. "Uh oh, there goes my reputation, the drive-up of shame." She joked.

"She doesn't like me very much." I parked beside Luna's truck.

"Why? Have you had sex with everyone that works here?"

"Not yet." I laughed. "No, I kind of accused her of something. I don't know. I don't remember much, but I sort of went crazy in the store."

"Hmm. Well, I'll see you around." She got out of the car without looking at me, yelled something to Pink Lips, and then got into her truck. I went into a daze, unable to appreciate what had happened to me. For a mere sixty dollars, I got drunk, fed, and laid. Then she left me without any Velcro-promises. But I still felt as empty as ever.

I drove off toward Floyd's property, deciding to get some work done while in the area, but in my daze, the brake wasn't touched and I ended up way out in the country, reflecting off into fields of yellow, wanting to stop off at the mom and pop stores to get a drink, but then remembering I didn't have a nickel to my name. A traffic light turned red and Clapton played on the radio as I stared blankly at the gas gauge on empty. The light turned green, and it hit me that I needed to get home before the gas ran out.

After making it to Central Avenue, a sputter from the muffler made my heart stop. She kept on going, but it couldn't be long before the red flash crippled into a dead star. One more spurt. I pulled into an empty parking lot beside a used car business. When my foot left the gas, Charlie began to shake until she just clunked to a stop. The empty lot surrounded a bank that was out of business. It was a rare sight. I tried to focus on the ground and then on a miniature golf course across the street. My mind knew of the used car dealership, and it even had some unthinkable thoughts. Charlie wasn't an expendable possession. She was a companion of adventure. I walked away. I needed another plan. I needed help. It was an emergency. The end of a rope, as they say.

Luke wasn't an option. My mom wasn't an option. It would have to be Alex. It was time for me to let him down. He could spare just a few dollars, maybe wire me a twenty, maybe a hundred. He was working in a bar in Brooklyn, I'm sure he was making thousands, and I have sent him at least a thousand dollars worth of books and music, yes, a hundred would be like asking for pennies. I could send him my essays once I touched them up, once I started them, once I finished them, yes, that would be the best move. He could sell them to one of the millions of magazines up there. Who knows how much the New Yorker pays for such potential genius? He could just keep the profits off the mere hundred dollars. What an investment! My spirits were awakened, my chemicals mixing with my decisions, my shameful ideas turned inside out. I would finish my masterpiece that day, then get it to him as soon as he sent the money, yes, things had to happen for me soon, otherwise I'd have to wait out another ten minutes.

My neighborhood surrounded me like bullies pointing, laughing, and kicking dirt in my face. A grumble came from my stomach, different than the sharp pain of hunger. I thought about how long it had been since I'd been to the toilet. Probably since the last time I was drunk. I made it home, just beating out my digestive tract. *The Moron Factory* notebook was still beside the bed on the floor. I swiped it up as I shuffled to the bathroom. My whole apartment was unusually hot. Even the toilet seat was like plastic melting. I read over the pages. It could be described as a sickly-nervous paranoid perspective of a refrigerator magnet. Those fucking New Yorkers would eat this up. It would be perfect for those goddamn cosmopolitan bastards. I'm pretty sure they love anything they can't understand, all sunrise diners with hipster slummies over the speakers.

I wrote at the top of the first page: ALEX, DON'T CHANGE A THING EXCEPT EVERYTHING, AND PLEASE DON'T TAKE AWAY THE RIDICULOUS, IT'S ALL I HAVE LEFT! Then dated it, SEPTEMBER 22 like I hadn't missed a step in life. I couldn't tell you the day or the year, but I knew very well that it was September 22. Boy, did it feel good to sit there on that toilet. There was something about the bathroom that possessed tranquility. If I married Luna, it would be where I would write everyday just like Kerouac did when he was forced to marry that gal he knocked up. It reminded me of Woody Guthrie. He said, "The more you eat, the more you shit." It's all that crap we put into ourselves day to day, and I'm not talking about food. It's the past. We get full on the past, constipated on the past, delusional on the past, cowardice on the past.

When I came out of the bathroom the dust seemed to have taken over the air. There just weren't enough possessions in my two rooms to suck in the dead. Our microscopic skin cells, our moments of madness, our accomplishments, our dreams, our possessions, our memories, and so on, become a layer of gray over a bookshelf, waiting to go to a rag, waiting to go back to the soil, fertilizer for our own cemetery plots. I took my phone card and went to call Alex.

A mechanical voice through the payphone tried to tell me how many minutes were left on the card, but I blocked it out. That would be a good invention for Floyd's wife, an alarm clock that told her how many minutes in life she had left. Then she could go around the world with a set of jumper cables, helping other humans get to work, get to the beach, get to a date. Then again, if she knew she would probably just sit in front of the TV with a gallon of ice cream and a vibrator.

On the fifth ring, Alex answered. I was shocked. He never answered his phone and I had gotten so used to leaving messages or talking to him cosmically that it was a bit awkward at first.

"Hello?"

"Alex! It's me."

"What's up man?" He always acted as if the sky was falling and he was already wearing a steel hat. But nothing was up. There was just something that needed to be said.

"Nothing is up, nothing at all." Then we were silent for a while, for a few seconds. There was a kid with a chocolate dipped cone. I could tackle the little bastard and take it from him. It would teach him a good lesson about life. The question of money was on the tip of my tongue. "I wrote this essay and it seems pretty good. I'm going to send it to you, maybe you can do something with it."

"Cool."

"I titled it, The Moron Factory. What do you think?"

"It sounds pretentious, it sounds arrogant like all of your titles." He laughed. It was true. I had written more titles than checks and love letters combined.

"I refuse to give in to making people feel comfortable. It's useless."

"Yes, uselessness?" He hesitated. "Did you edit it, or even read it?"

"No man, that's not what I do, you know that. If I start questioning and fixing anything in my life, that means I'm living *your* life or some other fucking robot life. You can edit it, make it pretty, it'll just sit under the mattress here destroying sleep."

"Sure man, that's great." He sounded as if he was staring at a girl's ass or something.

"I have this book I'm going to send also, it's..." I lost concentration, still thinking about the money. There was the last box of books back in the apartment with the one book that Alex had sent me.

"Are you alright?"

"Of course, the worse I get, the more the world makes sense, and the better I get, the more the world confuses me."

"So how's the world?" He asked.

"If it made any more sense I'd be a genius with two umbrellas."

"What are you doing for work, you teaching again?"

"I slept with this girl last night. I bet she's not even twenty-two, amazing girl, she's from the Motor City, and now she sells worms and cigarettes."

"That's my kind of job." We laughed. "How much does that pay?"

"You'd be a millionaire before you could say Cheetos-dick." Laughter. Silence. Ask him! I thought. "She started a conversation about God with me. Can you believe that?"

"I guess? Which theory did you give her?" Alex asked sarcastically.

"The one where God is me, God is you, inner voice and such."

"That's a good one, well, maybe not good, but at least it gives some kind of explanation of who you are." Alex said.

"What does that mean?"

"It means you are constantly following through with these ridiculous visions, so at least you have your God to blame them on."

"Listen Alex, you know me better than anyone, and what makes sense to me doesn't make sense to most people. What you see as ridiculous, I see as sensible. I am God. God is that brief moment in time in which everything makes sense. My life is just a series of ten-minute moments that always make sense." I was getting sort of defensive.

"So everything that you do makes sense?" He asked in a condescending tone. It was how Alex came across sometimes, because he was supposed to be superior in his mind.

"I don't know man, it doesn't matter if it makes sense. I can't stop myself from doing whatever it is, mainly and probably because I don't want to stop. And I'm quite aware of what's going on, but controlling it is a whole other thing. It's like the wind. I know it's there, I know where it stems from, but putting on a goddamn parka won't explain it or stop it."

"I know you have an understanding with the voices in your head. Sorry I called them ridiculous."

"Don't be sorry. If they weren't ridiculous to you or say my mother, then what the fuck would I do?" *What the fuck would I do?*

Alex said something that I didn't hear. What the fuck would I do? Just ask him. "So do you think you could sell the essay, I mean find a magazine for it, a publisher?"

"Sell it? Shit man, you know essays don't pay, that's kind of the point."

"No, I didn't know that. But it's not about money." I can't believe that came out of my mouth. "It could also be turned into a story. You could turn it into a story."

"Okay, just send it to me. Stories don't pay either though."

"I thought you were around all those literary types up there? What the hell do they do for money?"

"Work menial jobs. I'm surrounded by all the supposedly right people, but that doesn't mean shit either, they don't know what the hell they're doing either, they don't know just like... Look man, you just need to come up here and get out of your trap."

"This is my home, New York would tear me apart."

"Yeah, but it would tear off all the right pieces."

"Listen Alex, I'll know when to leave, God will direct me, it will be easy. So when it comes, it will come."

"God is that brief moment in time in which everything makes sense." He repeated my saying, possibly in jest. "That sounds good, write that down."

"Ah Alex, you're the only one in the world who humors me, everyone else just learns one thing from me, which it turns out is how not to end up like me..."

"You mean end up hearing voices?" He was fucking with me in his horrible egotistical way.

"Oh, I hear the voices of millions, you have no clue, I hear your voice all day, it's always questioning why you're turning into an asshole, a phony artsy asshole."

"You know what your problem is?" He asked me as if I didn't know what all my problems were. "Or at least one of your problems? You don't have the capacity to speak to others about things that don't matter. Can't you once just have a goddamn conversation about the weather, or the game, or just how you feel?"

"Alex, now listen Alex, I'm the only person on this planet that pushes you to stay true to yourself, everyone else is convincing you to be them. And do you know who tells me to tell you this shit?"

"The voices?"

"Goddamn right!"

We laughed shortly.

"All I'm saying is that you've done the scary weirdo genius thing." Alex said. "You are an Arcane original. Up here you'd be a dime a dozen, and you're scared of that."

"Thanks Alex, you're one hell of a confidence builder."

"Just fucking come to New York. Christ man, I have work for you, a place to crash, I mean, I'm broke and scraping by, but shit, that's what you do, right?"

My heart sank. Then my head floated in joy. Thank God I didn't ask him for money! What a fool I would have looked, asking my poor friend for a hundred dollars?

"Why didn't you tell me you needed money? I'll send along some cash in the book, and of course if you can sell the essay, you can keep whatever. Sell it for a million and take some expensive whore out, eat caviar off her tits."

"I'll be just fine thanks," he chuckled. Cocky bastard. "But you man, you and the world, every time I actually talk to you, it's the same shit, you're stopping yourself, you put boundaries on your reach, I mean to be completely honest with you, you are a complete moron most of the time. If you actually got in that Sunbird and drove north, you'd end up in the Pacific Ocean. You need the devil's escort, something more disastrous than yourself."

"Oh Alex, you're one to analyze. All you do is move from one city to the next, thinking that you're becoming more cultured and sophisticated and educated by the world, but you're the fool forgetting that it doesn't matter. You don't have the courage to be an absolute nobody."

"You're right and it is something of worth, but that doesn't mean you shouldn't challenge yourself."

"Sure, sure, hey listen to this!" I searched through my notebook looking for this quote. It took a second or two.

"Shit! Hey, I have to call you back. I'll call you right back." He hung up. He wouldn't call me back, because he didn't know about my phone situation. But either way, I was elated that he was broke also. I cursed myself for being so stupid, for actually considering asking a friend for money. All of my capitalistic life was a mistake of some sort, taking money from the devil, rejecting my Grandmother's small inheritance, turning down jobs, asking friends for loans in my mind, burning twenty-dollar bills to spite fat record store clerks, and so on. I needed to get off my nutso chair and take some bizarre action, fly back around the world and turn my life inside out. Alex and I were like brothers and there's no way I'd let him pull the weight of our cosmos. Giants in the form of buildings, ego contests, and crossword puzzle tongues already surrounded him. Maybe he was right about challenging myself in the way that society expects? Maybe? Who the hell was ever right? Well, either way, first thing was first. A little money would be needed, just a jump start to get my shit together, yes, money, gas, job, catching up on the Sisyphus Project, and then go back to Luna a real man.

The remainder of my books was packed away in the last of my boxes. I rummaged through the novels, trying to find a book to send Alex. A promise is still a promise, even if it came through a "complete moron's" mouth. *A Moveable Feast* was floating near the top. Hemingway and Fitzgerald's characters always reminded me of Alex and myself. I flipped through the pages, checking for excessive highlighting. If the pages were clean, I would have to sell it to Hans. Luckily almost every page was decorated like a Christmas tree. I put it to the side with *The Rosy Crucifixion* and *The Moron Factory*. I realized how organized my brain seemed at the time. I did some math equations in my head, tried to think of my third grade teacher's face, thought about opening a savings account, and then cleaned up the broken scotch bottle glass on the floor. Maybe Alex was my therapy, my reasoning that an artist doesn't have to fulfill a misanthrope's fist. I took a knife and carved the word FREE into my coffee table, and then took it out to the curb along with some other extraneous items. The sky was growing gray. It was time for the late afternoon thunderstorm. There was an urgency coming from the chirping of the birds. I would have to hurry if I wanted to get the books over to Hans. I rushed back inside to get the box, but the sound of a large raindrop splashing against the aluminum awning made my motivation weak. The box crashed to the dirty carpet. I went back outside. The clouds had seen me. My great father was teaching me yet another harsh lesson. He knew that humans adapt to love and nature. Instead of dealing with the heat, we invented air conditioning, instead of just having sex, killing, and existing we invented sophisticated fetishes, sewage systems, and blenders. I, instead of looking to the god in the sky from my window, I put a garbage bag over the box and followed the sidewalk to the bookstore. It would be a solid two-hour walk. The rain slowed and the lightning began. I screamed, "Give it to me! Right down the spine motherfucker!" It was almost a song. Two boys on bikes rode up beside me. One said, "Weirdo." They laughed. Maybe a truck will hit them? I hoped. Maybe a truck will hit me?

I got up to Central Avenue and the box felt like a thousand pounds. I took shelter under the Dairy Queen overhang, and watched the trickle go into a downpour. Across the street, Sign Guy was under the awning of a thrift store. APPRECIATE RAINY DAYS, APPRECIATE YOUR ROOF. He waved at me. I waved back. There was another man waiting out the storm by the pickup window, but he wasn't looking at the rain. He was completely focused on his ice cream cone, as if there were a strategy involved, as if the fate of the world lay in his sticky hands. I kind of respected it. He was so into it that I don't think he realized I was there. A lightning bolt struck down through a telephone pole across the street. A spark popped from the power lines and the block went dead. That caught his attention. "Holy shit?" He told himself.

"Holy shit is right."

He looked over at me with a smudge of chocolate over his mustache and left cheek. "Shit man, where'd you come from?"

"That's a long story." I held back the obscure answers and just went straight into lies. "But the short version is my car ran out of gas on the way to this bookstore. I have a reading tonight and these are my books. I was going to catch a taxi, but there doesn't seem to be any around." A city taxi passed, but he didn't see it. "And even if one did, they couldn't see me from way back here." I couldn't believe my nerve. Who tells such lies for no reason?

"So you're an author?" He said behind his cone.

"You could say that. Do you read literature, poetry?" I prayed for a no.

"Um, the newspaper, and once I read a book from that horror guy, what's his name?" While he tried to think, I plotted.

"Is that your truck?" There was only one pickup truck in the parking lot.

"Yep. What's his name, you probably know? Shit."

"You wouldn't happen to be going downtown? It would be a saintly act if you could give me a lift, just down the road, I'd ride in the back of course, just two miles down Central, very easy ride."

He didn't care either way. "Yeah sure, I'm not going that way, but shit, it'd be an honor to have a real author in my truck. Hey, maybe you could put me in one of your books?"

"Yeah, maybe. You have a face that deserves to be put into words."

So he finished his ice cream and we ran out to his pickup, him in the front, and me in the back. The man drove like a maniac. The back of the truck skidded every time we hit the low part of the rollercoaster road. I hung on without really caring what would happen to me. Even a laugh came out at one point when my body bounced off the bed and I slammed against the side. The cranking driver hydroplaned into the empty strip mall. Hans would think I was the biggest idiot in the world, if he didn't already. Maybe that would scare him into giving me more money.

"There ain't nobody here?" My driver hollered through the back glass.

"It's an after-hours thing, invitation only." I yelled back, jumped out the back, and grabbed my box. "Thank you for the ride."

He cracked the window. "Hey, can I have one of your books?"

"Yes, of course, soon, very soon." I walked away.

"But I don't know your name?"

"Stephen King!" I answered the wrong question as usual.

When I got under the covered strip mall walkway, I waved him off. "Thank you!"

He pushed his farmer's baseball cap up and then back down again. Then the truck went into reverse as if an angry man was driving it. Hans was looking at me through the glass. Boy, I was soaked. I took my shirt off and shook like a wet dog. Hans was still staring. I waved at him, but he wouldn't acknowledge his best customer, the charitable buffoon with a garbage bag of literary treasure. I rang out my shirt. The water splashed down beside the metal donation box. "You will not get any of my books tonight." I told it and vowed to find any of my books in the store that I donated last time. It would be a thorough investigation. I would bring this children's literacy scam to a halt! I laughed out loud and waved at the staring bookstore owner again. He picked his hand up, but didn't really move it. After the dripping had stopped, I put my shirt back on and went inside. "Listen Hans, I know what this looks like and I assure you that there is nothing normal going on. I have a small treasure out there just waiting to be unburied, minimal highlights, just like you love, customized for you Hans."

He looked at me like a monster. "Well bring them in, I'm not going out there!"

"Yes, how foolish of me."

I ripped off the garbage bag and brought the box in. "I'll just look around while you do business." I said. He nodded without really moving his head. Then he looked up at me suspiciously. Maybe he knew of my secret investigation? "I'll just look around?"

"Please do." He said, annoyed.

"Thank you, thank you." I felt like such a psychotic worm. Why did I thank him? Why twice? Why did this man make me feel so desperate? He was just a kind and gentle soul of a past world. Maybe it was the way he looked at each book with his glasses on and then off as if to get a clear view, then a blurred view. It was genius. I don't know?

My investigation began. The first of my books I recognized was *The Idiot*, but it turned out to be one of the minimal highlighted. I flipped through the pages and realized it could have been decorated much more than it was. I glanced down at Hans. He had taken a specific interest in a first edition copy of *Book of Dreams*. A ghost gave it to me, so I didn't mind parting with it. He opened it, studied the cover, put it at different camera angles, put his glasses on, and took them off. He looked down the aisle at me looking at him. "Old friends." I told him. My investigation continued a little more arrogantly. The Kerouac gem gave me a push. But either way, I truly couldn't remember the ones he had bought and the ones I gave away. It didn't matter; I was starving, hungry for something bigger than what the world had to offer. Alex was right. I needed to challenge myself.

"Okay." He said, meaning okay, take your books and get out. I went up to the counter and noticed the box was empty, which was a good sign. "This is what I'm going to do for you friend, but only because I know you have problems." He put his hands on two piles of books. I couldn't believe he called me friend. "This pile I'll take for two dollars a book, this pile, like last time is too marked up, but I'm going to buy it for a dollar a book and donate them myself, mostly because you are walking home, right?" He asked me, but nothing registered. I just stood there trying to figure out what problems he was referring to. I couldn't think of one. "You're walking in the rain, right?" He repeated.

"Yes, I'm sorry, yes."

"Fine then, so that's that. Then there is this," He held the *Book of Dreams*. "Which is actually worth something. I'll give you seventy-five for it, and with the rest, that comes to..." He punched his calculator for my benefit. "One hundred and three."

The number clicked in my head, and I'm not sure how much I expected, but definitely not that much. "Ah Hans, you're a saint, a real live angel. I'll take it... friend."

He actually smiled after seeing the joy he created. He gave me the cash and we shook hands. Tears started to well up in my eyes, and I rushed out before he saw them, waving with my back to him. What a saint that Hans! Surely he was going to be up there with Peter and Gandhi.

The rain splashed against my face, tingling rivers flowing from heaven and Mars and battery-powered clocks. My pace was furious. I must have blazed through the first half of the walk in fifteen minutes. I wanted beer and maybe some food. I had those nachos the night before. God, that seemed like years before. My stomach was shrunken and in the mood for liquids. But in the convenience store I grabbed a hot dog along with a twelve-pack. The total was $8.38. "Keep the change." I told the silent man behind the counter. He looked at the ten dollar bill and stomped his foot. I walked out gaily, engulfing the hotdog, and thinking about how that was probably the first tip he had ever made. "Gratuity! Gratitude shining!" I told the rain.

I made it back to my house in record time, even running at one point, luckily falling in the grass when my foot just stopped working, but I got back up with a streak of mud over my side and a slight limp. While I worked on the twelve-pack, I put together the package for Alex. My mind was still on Luna. My heart hurt when I thought about killing her off. She would never stay with me. Meeting people is so tragic, and falling in love with their nakedness is as close to the slaughterhouse as humans could get. I finished off the package with a letter:

Dear Alex,

By the time you get this letter, I will be a changed man. I will have changed my mind about everything I'm about to say, even though I don't know what I'm thinking yet. It's sad to think that nothing I feel will be a part of me anymore. It must be nice to think or even know that you are going to feel the same for the rest of your life. It's ideal, really. It's like you, a half-blind idealist. I'm not judging you. I know you know how to be a realist. It's admirable, your defiance. Anyway, I got laid some hours ago. I told you this on the phone, and even seemed happy about it, as far as I remember. The touch of a woman is exactly how the bible made it out to be, a secondhand apple from a serpent. I could have lived off of oatmeal the rest of my life until that goddamn apple showed up, or even, every evil fruit that has ever entered my life. It should happen again soon, and it'll be one more step toward complacency. Don't let it happen to you, don't get complacent, if not for yourself, for me. God, listen to me. I'm not talking to you. I'm talking to me. I can't get away from me. I'm here all the time. I'm hopeless. I'm drunk. I love life too much to see you be like everyone else. It makes no sense. I'm drunk. This is gibberish. What you're doing makes sense. Just look out for apples. I'm going to drink twelve beers tonight and attempt to write one decent sentence. Thirty-three years and I haven't written one thing I could die over. I settled to know that God and her ants have laughed upon my life. Maybe I should come up to New York. Maybe I could sleep in Central Park. That would make me feel good, I think. Just like you said, my biggest fear is that there will be thousands of others like me, pretending to sleep, dreaming, shivering with smiles on their faces. Then it will all be for nothing. It'll all be for nothing. Man, that rings in my head too much. Anyway, like I said, by the time you get this I will want you to move to an orchard in Washington. But for now, stay away from apples, kill your idols, and only eat when you're starving. Your most moronic friend in the universe will be doing the same...

the gleaming ocean of maybes lingers off my front porch...

Day 12,309

Floyd's alarm clock woke me the next morning. My head was as clear as it had ever been. Hot dogs and beer could be the key to life. It was going to be a productive working day. I could tell by the way the birds were singing, miniature flutes blowing the Earth around the sun. There were days like this in the past with scraped knees, sweat sticking to the pavement, a curfew for the day, a trickle of a creek, a string of bright blue eyes; in short, stacks and stacks of plastic details. Yes, it was all there with the hope that it would stay like shadows at dusk. Floyd's screen door creaked open and then slammed shut. It was as if my senses had been laced with steroids. I went out to bother him.

"It's a good morning for a cigarette. Mind if I join you?"

He looked at me with a short-lived disgust, and then handed me an abnormally long cigarette. "You're behind in the work." Floyd flicked his lighter up to my face. I took the hint.

The smoke burned my throat, but I held it in. "Yes, but today, today is going to be very productive. It's going to be a phenomenal day for work."

"You know, if you get the list done soon, I got some..." He finally looked at me as a person. "You don't do anything else do you?"

"If you mean for pay, no, I don't do anything else. I just get by."

"Well, in a few weeks I've got some contract work with actual pay, if you're interested?"

I couldn't believe that son of a bitch was trying to get me to work for money. Then he could charge me rent without the guilt.

"Floyd, I've never told you this, but I have a lot of money, I mean, a lot of money. It's just… it's just nice to be able to work for shelter. There's something primitive and earthy about it, like an indentured servant or a cripple's leg brace. I just need it." I puffed on my cigarette like it was a cigar. "But I would love to do the work, the contract work that is, it will probably be a nice change." I could tell Floyd didn't believe me about having money. I did have like a hundred dollars. That was all he mentioned of the work. He either really hated me or loved me. Fine lines always baffled me.

"Heard two people having sex the other night. Was one of them you?" Floyd asked as if he was churning iron.

"Yeah, it's been a spell, glad you got to listen in, good times..."

"You don't know a spell. Get married, and you'll know what a spell really is." He took his last drag and glanced back at his front door. "Anyway, that's what they make the Oriental parlors for."

"For getting married?"

"Mmm..." Floyd walked back inside his house.

I squinted my eyes and looked over the small yard, wanting a sprinkler to appear, maybe a slip-and-slide, maybe a swing set, but it was just a garden full of dying tulips. It was time to be present, time to get a real day's work in, complete with gallons of sweat, calluses, and shin scrapes.

The bus was as full as it had ever been. I stood, holding on to a metal bar along with two other men. Every so often one of them would accidentally look right at my beaten mug. My face still boasted light purple streaks that shot down from the inside corners of my eyes. Soon it would be gone, and only a blurred memory of chaos would be left behind.

The bait shop came up faster than expected. All of a sudden I became very nervous. I had money again and it was all I needed if the system was still intact. But tragic women were a dangerous breed, and Luna would crush me when I let her. There would be no choice until the aftermath. The parking lot didn't have any pink lipstick cigarette butts, so I took a deep breath and went inside. She saw me and we played a game of not noticing each other. I scanned over the aisles, randomly picking up snack foods and putting them back in the wrong places.

"You're screwing up everything." Luna told her only customer.

"It was already a mess, rows, schemes of convenience and such." I said into a bag of chips.

"Not that. I mean you're screwing up the one-night-stand. The concept of fucking and never seeing each other again."

"When a man needs worms, he can dig into the soil, but when a man needs gum he must dig into his pockets." I grabbed another 25 cent pack of gum. "Anyway, I fell into a pile of money and thought maybe you'd want to make it a two-night stand. You could fall in love with me and I'd never buy gum from this establishment ever again."

"Never?" She said, and we finally looked at each other.

"Yeah, that's right."

"Only if you promise."

"Promise." I held up a bag of nuts. "I swear on these nuts."

She didn't laugh. "I work until eight tomorrow, come pick me up, just like last time."

"Sure, tomorrow at eight."

She smiled and mimed out a *yes*. I left the store with eyes over my shoulder as if someone was playing a trick on me with a baseball bat. But the world was in order at the moment, and no one hit me.

It was still early by the time I reached the tool shed, probably several hours before noon judging by the shadows. I began right away by chain sawing a massive pile of trees. It felt right, everything, the sun, the flies, the way the chunks of wood flew up around my face. Life was definitely melding into the way it was supposed to be, whatever that means. Maybe it means that you are connecting with the universe from your world, your country, your community, all the way down to yourself. We're all becoming one.

The metal teeth ripped at the bark and the veins of the dead wood. I began chanting, "Chop that wood, carry that water, what's the sound of one hand clapping!" Then I got the insane idea of cutting my leg off and watching myself bleed to death just like the trees. Would it matter? Nothing would stop my disappearance. I would not make a sound! No, everything would stay the same, that one big bubble that everyone is trying to float in. "Enough!" I yelled to the voice. Life was good. Life was coming together. I was almost in the bubble, the scheme of iridescent forgetfulness, all that love that fills up red balloons and pops and lingers in the ozone, giving us a beautiful cancer of the soul. "Did you not almost starve yourself to death?" It was all a game if one was willing to play along. Could I be that arrogant to think I was outside the game while still possessing happiness? Oh, the gleaming ocean of *maybes* lingers off my front porch.

Before I realized it, the sun had passed over my head and was looking at me from the west. There was a week's worth of logs chaotically stacked waiting for a match or a rainstorm. I called it a day. I went back to the bait shop to pick up a drink and talk to Luna, but unfortunately, my nemesis was there with a smile, an evil smile. I grabbed an apple juice, crackers, and a jar of peanut butter, just out of spite. I hadn't eaten all day, but felt good otherwise. It was the power of a good day's work and the expectation of a woman.

I made sure to put down a twenty-dollar bill. "I'll take all of my change this time." I told her. "Gratitude is the root of gratuity, and gratuity shines. You have many irreplaceable qualities, but that is not one of them."

Pink Lips didn't say anything back to me. She just stood behind the counter with that damn grin as if she knew something I didn't know. This was the lowest point in my life. I had a job, shelter, a woman, money to buy food, and a perfectly healthy colon, yet this awful human being in front of me knew something I didn't.

"This is not the end." I put my finger in her face, and then walked out to head toward home.

There was a local music magazine lying on an empty bus seat. I picked it up and looked for something interesting to do with Luna. The next date should be different than the last. I needed to express something that we had never felt before, something of a perverse, pacifying nature. I didn't care if she ever wanted to see me again. What I mostly wanted was to make sure that she walked away with my skin under her fingertips. There had to be music. Yes! Music! If anything could show her the decent and calm and pure animal that existed within me, it was music. It must be true what they say about the beast. Unfortunately, Arcane didn't breed enough beasts to attract more than a handful of soothers. There was an old country singer named DC playing at The Neighborhood Puddle. He was an outlaw redneck turned wrinkled redneck, bound to play small rowdy bars the rest of his life, bound to sing all the songs that made him infamous, and bound to look back on the good old days after every show. The bar was relatively near my house, so I went and picked up two tickets. I couldn't wait to get rid of this money. It was a burden, a means to the future that I didn't care to have. It meant as much as the past, a distant dream of useless acts. Everything leading up till now would only prove to be a confused man who ultimately was living to write a poem and singularly fuck the moon one more time. If there was anything else in life, I wasn't sure of it.

 The next stop after getting the tickets was the grocery store. The fluorescent lights usually had a deafening effect on my common sense, but nothing could penetrate my brain that day. My internal list shot out clearly, told my feet where to walk, told my eyes where not to look, told my hands what to grab: two pounds of ground beef, peppers, onions, cheese, fancy crackers, and a bottle of good grocery store Cabernet. And there were the other clear thoughts that told me that everything was wrong, so I fixed them. I picked up frozen pizzas and put them with the cereal, there was dish detergent that absolutely had to be in with the asparagus, there was soup that needed to be between the ice cream and the TV dinners. It just had to happen. The world was out of order, and I would come back as a frog or a rental sofa if I didn't follow through with my duty. A man wearing jeans and a black jacket equipped with a plastic badge followed me for some time. I'm not sure why, it wasn't his business to maintain food order. He was waiting for my big move, but I didn't have one, just a bit of organizing.

I went to check out. The cashier began to ring in my items. The security guard went around the exit side and then confronted me.

"Excuse me sir, may I check the items in your bag?" He asked about my bait shop bag.

"Only if I can go through your pockets." I counted my money worrying if I had enough.

"I'll pull out my pockets to let you see what's in them." He was a major motion picture negotiator, very slick, coy, and useless. If there's one thing I can't stand, it's humans that take themselves seriously.

"Deal." I tossed the bag at him.

"$32.95." The cashier popped her gum. I handed her forty and figured there was around forty-three dollars left. I still had to get gas for Charlie. The cashier gave me my change and the security guard gave me my bag. He walked away without showing me what was in his pockets. It wasn't part of the reorganization. I was just proud of myself for preparing with food. Since Floyd offered me that job, I figured I could live off my emergency credit card until then, which was clearly the right thing to do. Who the hell goes around starving themself, selling off their only possessions, and living like a bum when they had credit. It was like Alex said, I was a complete moron. All these magazine revelations made my walk home more like a horse ride off into the rising sun. I was full of nervous happiness. Something was bound to go horribly wrong.

if I had one original bone in my body, I would have bought a ceramic duck and thrown it in a pond...

Day 12,310

I slept in the next day, getting up at what seemed to be around ten in the morning. I made peanut butter crackers for my lunch. The only portable storage device I had was a plastic grocery bag. I placed the crackers in the bag, tied it up, and headed out for the bus. On the way out of the neighborhood, sitting right in the middle of the sidewalk, was a pillow with a piece of shit right on top of it like it was the king of the Milky Way. I stopped to give it a good study. Maybe it would jump up and do a little song and dance number or maybe it would tell me the secret of life is hidden away in the rectum? Either way, I knew it wasn't a good omen.

By the time I was out by the bait shop it was just past noon. Luna should have started her shift by then. When I walked through the old screen door, my eyes landed right on those awful pink lips. She gave me that same evil smile as the day before. I looked around, pretending to browse the candy bars, but really searching for Luna's presence. I thought she was probably in the bathroom or stockroom or running late. She was already fucking with my head. I could feel that awful lady's stare over me. I gave up and went to work. But still, my mind became obsessed with her absence. That damn piece of shit. Why would it be on a pillow? Who would do something like that? Was it Arcane's way of putting on a show? Some kind of performance art? Thank God I wasn't really a dog, otherwise I would have just sniffed around the pillow and took a piss on it. There was so much more going on here.

I went out to the tool shed and grabbed the goggles. There was a fresh layer of a snake's skin almost fully intact beside the shed and on the path. I hung my bag of crackers on a bent nail and sat down on a log. The woods were hazy and sick. My body became heavy with a daydream. There was a figure in the image of man standing on the edge of an endless body of water. There was no light, but there was a reflection in the water that lit up like a mirror on fire. There was nothing except an idea, a useless idea, an arrogant idea. The reflection on the water began to morph into the first and last miracle.

When I snapped out of the daze, my face was wet, and even though my eyes felt swollen, I couldn't tell if the moisture was tears or sweat. The snake's skin was still alive. Nothing really dies, it just keeps regenerating itself in the mind of man, laughing out loud at the ludicrous notion of existence, cycles of music and words and contradictions.

Who knows how long I sat there either daydreaming or letting Luna eat away at my mind. I decided to start the work, but then realized that there would be no way to eat my crackers without something to drink. I convinced myself, yes, something to drink and then a good day's work. That is the order. By then it must have been two or three in the afternoon. I got to the bait shop and noticed there were three more pink-stained cigarette butts than before. If only I could focus on everything else in life this way. I shoved through the door and went straight for the beverage cooler with purpose, not even glancing at the identity of the cashier. Truthfully I was just afraid to look. There was a slight reflection in the glass cooler that showed me Luna. I quickly grabbed a soda and turned to realize the hallucination. Who created such things as reflections? We all should be blind and electric! Pink Lips could see the surprise in my expression. There was no way to hide my hatred for this woman. She played tricks like a half-wit magician, pulled dead rabbits from her cunt, turned her face from an angel to a highway billboard, and sawed herself in half when the head would have been the best trick. She took my dollar with some kind of weird satisfaction. I hurried out of the store to get back to the comfort of the snake's skin.

I was on edge about Luna. Maybe I had slept through the day again? Maybe it wasn't her fault? Sometimes when I can't wait to die, I realize that this world will die with me and that makes me sad more than my own nonexistence. So whenever I sleep through a whole day it makes me sad to know that the world didn't exist that day. What did they do that day? I imagined that all the humans just stood blankly on sidewalks, finally and truly unsure why did anything at all. This thought possessed me to where it was impossible to realize my time and place in the universe. The moment was being ground up into paper and hot dogs. I hated when I turned the truth around to keep the blame from others. But I really didn't know the truth of what had recently happened. I know I saw a piece of shit on a pillow, but the day escapes me.

When I got back to the shed, I went straight for the plastic bag full of crackers, blaming my delirium on hunger. Upon reaching my hand down in the bag, I found a colony of fire ants that had beaten me to my pills. Little red squiggles covered my hand, running up my forearm, looking for cover from the monster. I did nothing to stop them. The pounding of my palm was futile. They would just keep on marching. I felt bad for Luna. She must have been devastated, waiting outside in the dusty parking lot, smoking a hundred cigarettes, and using her clean air to curse me. How could I keep anything if the rising sun, the leftover smell of such a girl, and the ticking of a million blood cells couldn't wake me after eight hours of dreaming? I put a cracker in my mouth. I remember as a child, adults would proudly announce the protein source of insects. It didn't help, the laughter, the protein, the magnificent feeling of tiny legs squirming against my tongue. The first bite made me gag. I dumped out the rest of the crackers and just went to work.

A few hours later the forest was about to close for the night. I put up the tools and headed home. I was about to pass by the bait shop when a vision of my abandoned Charlie luckily came to me. It was a good time to buy a canister of gas, and even leave an apology for Luna via my favorite cashier. As soon as I walked in Pink Lips said, "She's not coming in, you can stop pretending to need stuff."

"What do you mean?"

"I know you're here to see Luna. You think you're some kind of Don Juan, but I told her all about you yesterday, about how you moved all those groceries around the store and how you started throwing things when I told you to stop, I told her about..." She went on a long rant of things I obviously did, but didn't recall. They sounded like things a complete moron would do. I phased out her curdled voice and realized that it was the correct day. I didn't dream through yesterday, Tuesday maybe? It was just the regular short rotation of the normal man. "...So imagine that? She doesn't show up for work today because she knows that an insane man would be by to stalk her. You're done bringing people into your miserable existence."

I didn't know what she was talking about. My existence was a playground of kids on amphetamines. I found a small plastic gas container. "I'm going to fill this up." I said, walking out the door.

She ran around the counter. "No, you pay first!" She said like I was going to try to burn the place down. I mean, honestly, yes, it did cross my mind, but lots of things float through my brain that never enter actualization. We were outside. She came at me with some kind of vengeance. It was off though, sexy and misplaced. I dropped a ten-dollar bill to the ground and she picked it up, losing her schizophrenic sexuality. Money is the enemy of passion. I think the container was eight dollars, so I put in a dollar's worth of gas, and left. Left furious by the way. No kidding, the thought of Luna thinking I was crazy actually made me crazy. It was self-realization of emotions that could only be produced from their own absurdity. The walk to the bus stop proved to be worthy of a gas-fume high. I stopped being angry and became dizzy, confused, and disappointed. Who needed drugs and booze when we have all these amazing substitutes for life? Gas, disappointment, and whims in the form of falling rocks... Mercy kept a good distance behind me, only catching up once a year, just to fall down in the dirt.

I passed by Willie's house. My stomach started itching inside. Thoughts of burning down his house ran through my fingers, luckily not reaching my feet. The ants had come alive through my digestive system. They bit the lining of my intestines, stomach, and then on up my esophagus. I bent over and puked out a little phlegm and then a lot of flaming gook right beside the red gas can. I saw my bus coming down the road. It seemed like a big rolling cloud, taking the angels and the oblivious off to another little world. The intricate design really could blow your mind if you thought about it too much. I waved the driver down because the stop was another hundred paces away. He stopped for me because I was usually the only passenger that far out. He gave my gas jug a worried look, but didn't say anything as I swiped my bus pass. I went all the way to the back, so the fumes wouldn't bother him. There was a sticky cola-like substance on the seat. I knew that gasoline was good for removing those types of messes, so I poured a little on the seat and rubbed the bottom of my shirt over it until it was gone. It felt good to help out my new favorite bus driver. I gave his mirror a thumbs-up. He didn't see me. The fumes were making me light in the head, giddy and frantic at the same time. I searched my pockets for a lighter or a match, but had neither. A burning cloud rolling downtown, catching everything it touches on fire. My fingers seemed to be numb. I felt saliva running over my bottom lip and into my chin hair. Everything was fine.

I could see my bus stop approaching, but my body had become part of another element. The gas fumes held me down and spun my thoughts. The stop came and went as I tried uselessly to move my arms. My red Sunbird held her ground by the broken down bank. When my chest and hands hit the dirty floor things got easier. The small crowd up front all turned to see the buffoon. The whole planet of Neptune floated in front of my eyes and in-between the rubber ridges. There was more or less a grain of sand, a wrapper from a toothpick, and a thousand agonizing smiles. The smell of being walked on replaced the fumes. I regained my senses and in a drunkard's motions scrambled to my feet and then back to my seat.

The bus had already passed the stop for my house also. I pulled the cord. The bell muffled out a ring, and before the rush could ever get from my head, I was walking in my front door. The odor was venomous. I began devouring the wine and cheese that Luna would have just vomited back up. There was so much to do, so much to think around before getting drunk, before getting light. It seemed there was a rainbow of contempt over my bibles. Who was she to judge? "Everyone is insane, everyone is sad, everyone is confused! Her words!" She was sad. I drank straight from the bottle and tried to forget. My shell was so thin. The slightest touch of intimacy could tear me in two. There were prophets with paperweight dreams, there was an electric surge between the ocean and the fog, and once we let go of thinking, then we could finally repair the rips in our skin and breath. The bottle of wine was strictly there to wash down the fancy cheese and crackers. Once they were gone there was no reason to remember what happened next. The promises are as lucid and reliable as a commercial for insurance.

But... there are facts, which is to say, moments in the memory that we perceive to be true. These facts presented themselves in the form of the tangible clues in my apartment the next day: an empty wine bottle, five empty beer cans along with an empty 40-ounce bottle, purple finger imprints around my biceps, a smoky shirt, pants' pockets turned inside out, and a dollar left on my floor.

I decided to go to the show by myself. The Neighborhood Puddle was almost a pint of whiskey away. In the alley beside the liquor store, I saw a body partially covered with a sign. I went in further to investigate. It was Sign Guy. He was dreaming, mumbling words meant for another world. The sign covering him read, DON'T BE FOOLED, KINDNESS IS SELFISHNESS. I put a twenty-dollar bill in his pocket. He mumbled some more words and turned over. His sign slipped down to the ground.

There were a few sips left in the whiskey bottle, so I stashed it in the back pocket of my jeans before getting to the theater. It would be useful later on, and since everything was working for me like shit on a pillow, it seemed best to use my whims instead of rationalism. This was the next journey of what is remembered. The bouncer was a replica of the bouncer who knocked my lights out at The Abbey. I gave him my ticket. "Do I know you?"

He looked me over. "Nah."

"Well don't worry, we'll be best friends before the night is over." I handed him my extra ticket. "Don't need this one, do what you will with it, it only brings me anticipation, and that's not good for anyone *really* living." There was something about him that comforted me, like he understood whatever I was doing, maybe better than I did. But truthfully, he didn't care. He just took the extra and gave me a familiar look, the kind without trust. A good rule is to never trust anyone who gives you something without asking anything in return, like a drink, a song, or a concert ticket. I was lucky, I didn't have any money to buy a drink and I couldn't carry a tune. Well, I did have a few crumpled up dollar bills in my pocket. Intrigue, alone, pulled out the bills. This hippie chick bartender, ready for a big night of rednecks such as myself came over to me with a face shield.

"Just water please, I don't drink soda." Boy, did I think I was witty. She went to get the water and I turned up my pint of whiskey. There was already an urban cowboy on stage, captivating several couples up front. I took my ice water and invaded the lash of mediocrity. The singer was only ten feet away. There was a short row of seats in the middle and wide aisles on the sides, and for some unknown reason there was pink tape blocking off the first three rows.

I looked over the small population of cowboy hats and found a hatless couple sitting down. I approached them. "Can you believe all these phony weekend cowboys?"

"Do what?" The guy asked me. His girlfriend had these engaging blue eyes. I had to look away.

"Just pointing out all the phonies in here. You guys seem to be the only ones in here that aren't wearing a belt buckle the size of North America or a mint condition Stetson."

"Yeah, I guess it's just a style more than a lifestyle now." He said.

The singer had on a pair of snakeskin boots. I took a slug off my bottle. "You're absolutely right, absolutely." I told him with a pat on the shoulder. "Hey! Can I buy you a drink, a shot, a beer, anything?" It took all of seven minutes for me to forget about all the lint in my pockets.

"No thanks partner, we're just fine."

They were genuinely nice people, so I decided to get away from them. If I knew me, then I'd rather be away from the nice ones. The guy on stage played his last song. We all clapped politely as he exited to the side. The theater began to get crowded. The more people that came in, the lonelier I began to feel. It got to the point where I was backed into a corner. It seemed like there were eyes all over me, but whenever I would catch one, it would disappear into the floor. There was desperateness in my soul. It needed some escape. It needed to create havoc, destroy the mundane mirrored walls; in short, this is where things got blurry. More bodies filed in, took up all the seats, and filled in the spaces on the sides. I was feeling sick, drunk sick, like maybe I was about to puke or get the hiccups. "Why do they have that tape up?" I asked no one in particular, but a guy turned to me and said, "I think he puts that up because there's always fights up near the stage when he plays."

"Yeah, that should do the trick."

The lights were turned down and the bodies came in closer. The skin of others touched mine and it made me uncomfortable as if a sweat transfusion was the first step to dying. My arms were pinned to my sides and someone was on my foot. It had to be over a hundred degrees in there. That voice in my head – the one in which the universe made sense, told me to explode, run, turn into a hurricane, but I was paralyzed. There was one tiny sip left in the bottle. It mixed half and half with my saliva. It told me it was time to write a poem. It told me that we never know when it's the last time we get to do what we want despite a warm bed. I pushed through the people in front of me like a wedge. There were some grunts, more sweat, drinks spilled, and the pink tape blockade. I pushed it down and stepped over it, all three rows to myself. The crowd began applauding and at first I imagined it was for me, but then I saw DC walking out of the side curtains. I sat down in the middle seat of the first row, a few feet from his microphone.

He looked down at me without any surprise, and then out to the crowd. As he sat down to play, our eyes caught. He told me without words that he was too old and tired to deal with me. His band started up. I stood up and we were practically face-to-face. He began to sing and it seemed his band was purposely drowning him out. A couple of voices behind me yelled, apparently wanting someone to sit down. I yelled back, "You stand up, you stand up for once!" My voice blended in lightly with the music. DC thought he was dealing with just another crazy drunk, but I was no alcoholic. I refused to be categorized when I could just as easily get drunk off tomatoes and words. My fists were clinched, as the voices behind me grew stronger in numbers. The song finished and most of us clapped and whooped, but some decided to take the break to get their obscenities across. Thoughts of pain crept into the world. Lightning bolts of fear shot through me. It felt like being alive.

DC started back up after tweaking his guitar strings. My friend and adviser from the door was all of a sudden beside me. He leaned over into my ear. "You can leave on your own, or I can help you out."

I thought about this proposition for a couple of chords and decided the latter would make more sense. "I think you know the answer."

He was calm. "Alright, you sure?"

"The thing is… is you're huge, but I have something that you can't handle." I don't even know what I meant by that. The minute or so went by like life rewinding a man who jumped off a building while a stadium of fans took pictures. The faces blurred by as my friend carried me off into the abyss. They laughed, pointed, mocked, yelled, poked, and waited for their turn to stone me. Humans like to feel justified when it comes to harsh situations. My broken knees were justification. Of course I yelled things back that did as much good as them yelling at me. My friend had me by the arms with a machine grip. He guided me along as a bumper to get his own gigantic body through. Someone punched me in the stomach. I laughed, "You wouldn't exist without me." It was amazing to be a part of such a fiasco of fearful animal behavior. I became giddy with what could happen next. "That's it?" I said to no one in particular, but the bouncer took it to mean him. He threw me against the exit door. It was an excellent chest-pass. I went to the floor. He picked me up, helped me through the door, and then helped me down to the sidewalk. "You don't get it!" I told him.

"No, I get it. We all have jobs to do. You just don't know when you're clocking in or clocking out."

How did he know that? I knew there was something about us. We were connected souls. He dropped the extra ticket beside my feet. "Thanks."

He sat down on his stool and pulled out a pack of cigarettes.

"You mind if I get one of those?"

He pulled out two and handed me one. I broke it in half and threw it to the ground. He shook his head.

"Do you still get it? I didn't win." It was past time to leave. The air was heavy and musty. There was a real storm on the way. I did the old one-foot-in-front-of-the-other thing until landing in my local corner store. Its blinding lights and line of coolers made me wonder if this was heaven, but it turns out the floor wasn't gold, just linoleum or white bricks or dried up paper towels. I grabbed the afore mentioned 40-ounce of malt liquor and lost two of my three dollars. I hated when I was so predictable, like whenever I bought beer after being way too drunk. If I had one original bone in my body I would have bought a ceramic duck and threw it in a pond. But I drank the duck and woke up in the backyard with a hangover and all those clues. Despite the situation, I felt pretty good. It was always nice to get some human contact.

the Idiotainical Period...

Day 12,311

The robins were just beginning to chirp. My tomatoes stared at me with contempt. They were almost ready, maybe two days before turning them into my world famous chili. I thought about adding something exotic like mangoes. "God! Bring me mangoes!" I've found if you pray out loud like we used to do at the dinner table, then God hears you. I don't believe God can read our thoughts. If he could read my thoughts, then we would both be to blame, and as far as I know, God is perfect, he is what has happened, he is what is going to happen without any regret, he is considered the only use, but we get it wrong all the time.

A layer of sweat congealed with the dirt on my face. I pushed up off the ground. There was a thumping sensation in my brain. It seemed as if it was about time I started obeying my whims. First thing was to breathe. I lumbered toward the front yard. Floyd was sitting on the porch smoking his hideously long cigarettes.

"Did you sleep back there?" He asked, knowing the answer.

"No, well, maybe, well… Floyd, there are certain truths in life, and one is if you wake up to see another day, it doesn't matter where you slept."

"So you slept back there."

"I *woke* back there Floyd, I woke back there."

"You going to the property today?" He demanded more than asked.

"Can I have a cigarette?"

"No."

"Yes, as a matter of fact, I have planned to do a fifteen hour day, sleep under the trees, and then do it again tomorrow. There are an excess of logs to make into chairs. Kid's chairs! Chairs for classrooms in Guatemala. Chairs without splinters, with high backs so the learned child can grow properly."

Floyd gave me that same shake of his head and grunted. He probably wanted to make wooden flutes for the goddamn Boy Scouts of America. They could line up in a small town parade in Ohio and blow for their parents and their girlfriends and their boyfriends. Floyd flicked his burning cigarette across the yard and got up to go inside. I watched the thin string of smoke rise from the earth, squinting my eyes to make believe it was a huge fire starting in a field. "Good day Floyd. Today will be for the children!" He had already disappeared, but by God, he would see, yes, he and all the others would see. That day would go down in history as the first day of the Idiotainical Period. I laughed at my word. It was a good word, something to write down and keep for the future, for whenever I needed to explain something that was unexplainable. Why is the sky yellow? Why? Well, that's easy, it's because we're in the Idiotainical Period, that's why. Oh yeah, then why is life so useless? That's easy my good man, it's because we have entered the Idiotainical Period. Now get lost!

I was completely mad, no longer a moron, just dangerous. I decided to use my last dollar and change on a large cup of coffee. That would start the period off with a bang.

I thought about a career change, maybe actually becoming a thief, a Robin Hood of Arcane. I would steal books and donate them to Hans' literary program. I would steal gold and pawn it for bicycles. Then give the bikes to the kids who wanted to run away from this awful place, but wanted to run away faster than their tiny legs could accomplish.

"Today is for the children." I told the clerk at the corner store.

"It's too early for your shit man." He was wearing a pair of red sweatpants.

"Do we know each other?" I wondered if he was also a runner like me.

"No, we don't know each other. I know you're a lunatic, and you know I sell you beer and probably shouldn't."

"You don't have to be so angry, considering we don't know each other." I noticed he wouldn't look directly at me. "I just wanted you to know, what I'm doing, it's for the children, and that's all. I won't be a lunatic today. I'll just shut up right now." I walked down the candy aisle and then yelled, "Because today is for the fucking kids!" I started stuffing my pockets full of anything that would fit, and then filled a large Styrofoam cup with coffee. He kept his eyes as far away from me as possible. I probably could have just walked out with the coffee too, but it had nothing to do with the Robin Hood theme.

"A dollar." Sweatpants boy told me.

"You'll see," I kind of whispered as a soothsayer might. "They will be dancing in the streets. They are the future, you know." A pack of gum came out of my pocket as I pulled out my last dollar. The gum hit the floor and it reminded me of Luna. As I walked away from the clerk, he told me, "Hey, you dropped your gum."

"Oh the gum. Yes. It just wasn't meant to be." I left it on the ground.

On the bus, there were two children with their mother, a boy and a girl, both younger than ten years as far as I knew about kids. I sat across from them feeling every bump from Central Avenue jolt up into my spine. My pockets were bulging out with my bounty. It was a good take for my first job. There was a beef jerky stick, peanut butter cups, licorice, a pine tree shaped car deodorizer, a chocolate bar, a pack of vanilla cookies, and a lighter. The boy caught my eye. He seemed to be older than the girl. He had that look of wonderment that dies with puberty, lives in naive toes, and placates under the reflection of black ties. I reached out the chocolate bar to him. His hand automatically retracted. The trust of youth was crushed by the teachings of adults. My mother always used to tell me to *be careful* and I can't say that I ever obliged this request on purpose. It would really disappoint her if she knew that this whole time her wishes had been ignored. The last thing I want is to let her down, so I will continue to always lie to her. It's always best to lie than to hurt. The bible definitely got that one wrong.

I extended the candy bar even further because I could tell the boy really wanted it.

"Excuse me, what are you doing?" The mother asked.

"Oh, it's alright. In my spare time I help run a children's literacy program in conjunction with a local bookstore." I still had the chocolate out for grabs, but she held back her son's hand. "And also, I stole some things this morning for the children. Not your children in particular, but in general, incidentally whatever children I happen to run into." I think that sounded bad, but not to her son. He went through her arm and grabbed the candy bar. She quickly snatched it from him. The little girl laughed in excitement. "We don't want it, thank you." The mom tossed it back at me.

"I'll just put it over here." I put all of the food on the seat beside them. "You can take it if you want or not. It's just my duty, and truthfully, I haven't figured out how to properly carry it out yet." I went to the back of the bus and stared out the window. Everything with me was an experiment without conclusions, dancing with the devil without dipping him, planting seeds without watering the ground, killing myself without bullets... The city disintegrated into the countryside. Eventually, I was by myself again. The family and the food had disappeared. It made me happy, like I had some purpose other than making people miserable. I can't believe that horrible woman from the bait shop told me such lies. What did she know? She knew about worms and pop culture. I began to get more visions of good deeds, becoming a real thief, no more of that small time shit. That past thought of sitting in a jail cell crept back into my intrigue, eating three times a day, regular sleep, and constant thinking and writing. It would be very fitting. I came from an orphanage jail cell, and there was nothing wrong with going back. But I could only accomplish it by getting caught on a big job, armed robbery or something cool like that. The thought held no pride, no weird analysis, nothing having to do with my current fever. It was really only the kind of freedom that a mad person could ever put underneath their hat. At least in jail they're smiling and they know for a fact that your name is #348 when they beat you. They feed you a sack of green beans, ignore that there's no toilet paper, find the ones whose hearts will change, and they know, they know that a bone will keep you in line, yet they still go home to their wives and husbands and frozen dinners and backyards and bubble gum and all that other stuff that we welcome once the dish is in sight. This is what haunted me all day as I moved logs in a manner in which only Sisyphus could ever appreciate.

 I plotted out schemes that were bound to work, great heists only told in 21st century stories. It helped the pain that my ten hours of physical labor produced. My body gave in and fell with two logs over my arms, all the way to the dirt. A bit of a red clay cloud appeared in between my nostrils. I saw a millipede wiggle past me. It had a leaf for a moment and then raised its glass to the other side of the world, which happened to be my forehead. There was no justice. The leaf was gone, ignored as if it was raised inside a trash bag. Clowns trying to squeeze through an alley made for emaciated judges. If one were to beat the system they'd have to embrace absurdity and serenity at the same time. I was by the shed, curled up and just a shell of what I used to be. The millipede was gone and just the leaf remained.

The dream of being a world famous cat burglar had thinned into a wish for a sober night's sleep. I tried to head home. The bus came rolling down from the pinpoint horizon. I swiped my pass and the machine made a beeping noise.

"It's expired." The driver said. He knew me, or at least, he knew of me, so there was no pity involved. There was more of a smudge of joy. I stood right inside the doorway with a blank stare. "It's a dollar." He said to the exhausted and uncertain man. "C'mon, gotta keep schedule."

"I had a dollar earlier, but…"

"Let's go buddy. Dollar or get off."

"I had a dollar before, before I tried to help the children."

I turned around and exited the bus. There wasn't much choice at that point. I walked back toward the woods. The sun was just as tired, ready to go find my shadow on the other side of the world. My next great heist formed in my desperateness. There was a stick on the ground that I broke off until it resembled the shape of a gun. I went to the parking lot of the bait shop and waited until it was empty. It seemed to be around eight, closing time. Those stupid pink stained cigarette butts were everywhere. Must have been a stressful day. She must have really broken a sweat being worthless. I couldn't wait to put the fear of death into her. My checklist was short. Make her cry. Make her beg for her life. Make her plead for mercy. Then I'll take the cash and something to drink, maybe some sort of fruit juice blend.

After the last truck pulled off, I stormed into the store with the stick-gun underneath my shirt. It poked out like a crooked 44 Magnum. I slammed the door shut. "Alright you fucking piece of dirt-shit, open the cash drawer and get on your knees!" It was just like the movies had taught me to rob stores. I was a regular pro. But something happened that wasn't in my big plans. Pink Lips began laughing at me, laughing hysterically as a matter of fact. She choked on her words. "You – holy shit, you – please tell me – you're not serious?"

"I'm fucking very serious! Now let's go." I was a horrible actor. My tone had lost momentum and she began laughing even louder. She pulled out a large bottle of pepper spray and said, "Okay, you shoot me and I'll shoot you." Then she laughed at her own joke. I wanted to smash her face in, teach her what truth was, what violence was, wrap my hands around her veiny throat, kick her in the cunt, stomp on her head, but I just walked out. She had me every time. Maybe I was supposed to marry this woman? No one had ever made me so angry before. It could have been love. But that disgusting laugh wouldn't do. I could have taken her life, but ultimately I was a pacifist, a masochist, and mostly a harmless nut job. Fuck! Maybe I was the only one truly afraid. I go on preaching about everyone else, but what if I'm the only wrong one. This depressed me, but also liberated my thinking. I could finally keep a microscope on distractions, develop an ego for youth, and ignore time in the way that one keeps up with it. Right then and there as I stared up at a flock of geese shaving the treetops, I decided to finally be normal. It was a conscious decision to live like others, give it a real shot, try to be happy in their way, be a part of an organism, the cogs, the wires, the air, the farce. So by the time it was seconds away from turning dark, I found a good soft spot beside the shed again. I think it was where I was resting before, but this time the leaf was gone.

the curtain rises, falls, and burns...

Day 12,312

I think I went to sleep immediately, because there were no memories of discomfort. But when I woke before dawn, the air seemed frozen, the ground a block of ice. My body was stiff like a corpse. I got up and began running in place to get warm. As I huffed out carbon dioxide, I noticed that there wasn't any steam from my breath. It wasn't cold out, it was just me. My legs moved like an over-oiled machine, pumping away, trying to get my blood flowing. Sweat beaded up on the surface of my forehead. Then it began to pour and before too long my body was soaking wet and I was freezing again. What kind of sick game was God playing on me? He answered my prayer to kill me in the most perverse way. I took off my wet t-shirt and worked well past sunup. The thought of my tomatoes being almost ready distracted me from any chill, any scrapes, and any laughing women. I was sure that they would be ready by the next day, or at least by the day after that. My options were out there. All I had to do was take advantage of them.

There was a credit card buried somewhere in the few possessions I had left. I could use that until Floyd's new job kicked in. This whole new scenario of getting in line excited me. I could use credit cards, work for a paycheck, join a racket ball team, marry old what's-her-name, open up a checking account, replace light bulbs when they go out, and whatever else is on the list. There was plenty of time to study the list while I let priorities jump the line. Charlie was still stranded. I would need a car if normalcy was going to be in the next chapter. It would take me about six hours to walk home from the woods and then another one or two to get the gas to Charlie. I didn't *really* know, so I just started walking. Turns out it took about five hours with some jogging in-between crawling.

On the way up Central Avenue a car pulled up beside me. It was my old boss from the restaurant, the one that kept calling about the uniforms.

"You need a lift?" He asked me, an obvious trap.

"No thanks, I need to stretch the legs."

"I've been trying to get in touch with you. Did you change your number?"

"Yes, too many telemarketers. But I promise I will get the uniforms back to you, I've been so busy on my book and my Sisyphus project, it's just been overwhelming."

"The uniforms? I don't want those back. I think I saw a homeless guy wearing our bartender uniform. It looked better on him than most."

That was confusing. "Then why were you calling?"

"I needed a delivery man. You seem like you would be good at that."

Of course I would be great at anything I set my mind to, but why particularly a delivery man? "Well, thank you, but as you can see I have my days already steadily filled. But thank you for thinking of me."

Those days, boy, those days passed by with so much unabashed and unchallenged regret. The seconds seemed like little thorn pricks that bled me without the courtesy of a shoulder tap. Just one drama after another, the curtain rises, falls, and burns.

"You sure you don't need a ride? You look like you're about to fall over."

"Thanks, but no thanks. This is just the way I walk, stumbling forward."

My ex-boss drove away, and I continued stumbling toward home.

I grabbed the gas can after a gloriously nauseating search for my credit card. Of course it was in the pages of *The Rosy Crucifixion*. The card was just a relic that was left over after my last attempt to stay in line.

Then my new adventure began, a wealthy man on the road in search of truth, on the road to rescue his loyal companion that happened to be an automobile. I tried to hold the gas can behind me so the fumes didn't get involved like the time before. But either way, the first act showed its fangs in the form of a strip mall bar. I needed to get some food. It was justified. An establishment that took credit cards. A man who hadn't eaten in over a day. I put the gas can by a newspaper stand right outside the bar. The doors led to a room fully equipped with walls starving of shame, the standard look of vintage with the price tags still hanging on, an array of beer signs, neon lights, and just plain sadness everywhere. There were several men staring up at golf on the televisions. I walked past them and grabbed a stool at the end of the bar. The bartender was a bubbly brunette, yet punctual. "What'll you have?" Bubbles asked.

"I'll take a beer, a PBR will work."

She knew exactly how to smile and fool the world. I played along just like all the other jerks at the bar. It was my new life. These men were my justification for drinking in the daytime. I was only going to have one with my food anyway. Bubbles popped my cap across the bar. "And I'll take a burger with bacon and cheese and whatever else you can throw on it. Thank you."

She put the order in and went back to conversation with the man beside me, who was obviously a regular. Anyone could tell that by his exact comfortable slump. He seemed to be working on one of those jumble puzzles in the newspaper.

"What was I saying?" She asked him.

"You were saying that you don't believe that evil is a source. At least that's what I assumed you were about to say." He had something wrong with him that I couldn't put my finger on.

"Take it easy fellow." She joked. "I'll tell you what I was saying, I was saying that we can either assume that our Christian based morals are right or we have to accept everything which is considered evil as being just what it is, not one-sided. Hold on. Did I say that right?" She paused in heavy thought. The subject impressed me. This is how normal people drink during the day, I thought, with theological discussions in between Flaming Freddy's Fajitas. Maybe I could be normal after all?

There was an obvious lunatic at the jukebox, playing an array of hair metal songs and also playing his own air guitar. The bartender's conversation faded off as my hand burrowed into my pocket and squeezed the credit card. I had an overwhelming urge to bend the card in half.

Bubbles must have heard my thoughts. She came over. "Another PBR?"

"Yes, please." I had downed the first one in three gulps.

She brought it over. "Do you want to pay as you go or start a tab?"

The question echoed in my head without an answer. All I could think of was when that awful pink-lipped cashier told me to buy something or get out. This is how it is and will always be. Eventually the powers from beyond had the credit card out on the bar top.

"I'll just keep it open." She quickly snatched the card. "My name is Heather. Just yell at me if you need anything."

"Thank you Heather." All of a sudden I lost my appetite. There was too much going on, too many frames, and too many bumps. Bubbles and Jumble randomly went back and forth, saying things I couldn't imagine they actually believe. I frantically wrote down everything from my head to my notebook. My essay on happiness was almost done. All I needed was a title to wrap it up with a nice little bow. Maybe the Idiotainical Period would work?

My burger came out. Bubbles placed it in front of me without eye contact, and then went back into her point that I had heard at least seven times already. "I still don't think there is a source of evil or good for that matter. There is the concept that puts itself out there for interpretation."

Jumble looked up from his newspaper. "But nothing can be validated that way. As reasonable animals we have to set these concepts in order to stay reasonable, avoid the products of perceived evil, chaos, misery, hatred." There was something about him. My tongue was itching. The burger was steaming, fries were cold, and the only thing I was hungry for was to put Jumble in his place, that is, hear my own voice, and have someone finally hear my voice! I needed to be heard!

"It's a convenience of fear, not reason." I was basically dictating what I just wrote in my notebook. "We're the only unreasonable animals. Every other creature on Earth does exactly what its supposed to do, survive until they die. We have to create comfort, and Gods, and lines of right and wrong, and theories to help explain life, and the word *happy* to give a goal to this so-called misery. But just as God or just as rights and wrongs do not exist without us, neither does evil. We are the source and the holders of the concept, created to give balance between the strong and the weak, made to give confidence to cowards. The source is the same as the image we were made in. And who's to say what chaos is," I waved my hand in game show host form in order to present the current chaos we were surrounded by. There were eight televisions in my sight, there were hundreds of chair legs, the air-guitar guy at the jukebox, several dozen bar flies swarming above the taps, a chicken wing on the floor, pictures of famous athletes, rectangle tables, round tables, a mass of logo-oriented doodads that had grown into the walls, and dozens of different glassware designed to represent the liquid inside. "I mean if this isn't chaos, what the fuck is? We're just used to this catastrophe called a sports bar. Imagine if an alien walked in here right now?"

"See." Bubbles said.

"See what? Just because someone agrees with you, doesn't mean you're right." Jumble was right, no one should ever listen to me.

"It would be if he agreed with you." She flirted with a laugh. I could tell she liked him. It wasn't the usual fake bartender laugh. I started to eat my burger, but it was disgusting, it was a waste. I just wanted beer, and became progressively jealous for each beer she put in front of me. My mind became obsessed with war-like thoughts. I needed to conquer Jumble and then conquer her. There was no point going on in life until this happened. I grabbed a cocktail napkin and wrote down something about the source and about God. The napkin floated in between my middle finger and pointer. The two flirted more secretively to keep me out and I decided to make my move. "It doesn't matter who is right or ahead or in agreement. There are so many of us out here rotating through life with opinions and theories and whatever else falls into the category of clever, deep, learned, yet almost everyone doesn't really have faith in what they're ranting about. It's great to talk about it, to impress your fellow human, but no one does anything. You hope it might get you laid or respect or a better tip, but if one's theories only go as far as his scent of toothpaste then that's where they will die. Then it's just another sequence of distractions." Everyone became awkwardly quiet. I tend to do that to rooms.

"We just want something to talk about while we drink. If we put a magnifying glass up to everything we did or said, of course it would seem stupid." Jumble said. His voice had changed from cool and dark to a man just thrown into the Idiotainical Period. He was right, and I didn't apologize. What if he was the future king of this period and I was the messenger? All he needed was to get the message to realize his calling, his awaiting throne, his endless supply of cheeseburgers and beer that came with the job. But he wasn't. He was just another guy at a bar, he was me, he was the men watching golf, and he was the guy playing the air-guitar.

I took the last two stolen items from my pocket, the lighter and the pine tree deodorizer. It drew some attention, but the conversation went toward sports instead of the messenger's tools. Bubbles reluctantly put my fourth or fifth beer in front of me. I sipped on it quietly and thought about alternate forms of communication. Maybe we're all just doing it wrong. Maybe we should have tried some kind of toe sign language. I needed to show them the other forms, so I flicked the lighter underneath the cocktail napkin with my final words on it. There wasn't much time left, the end was coming soon. I close my eyes and it disappears. I close my ears and every sound that ever existed no longer has a name. I hold my breath and a single flame spreads over Earth as if it was all just a dream.

It burned quickly, but Bubbles was quicker. She poured my beer over the napkin and my hand.

"You freaking moron!" She didn't like my new form of communication. It was smoke signals at a poetry reading.

"According to my friend Alex, I am a *complete* moron." I corrected her. She didn't smile. "It will come like a thief in the night, the heavens will disappear with a horrific noise, and the elements will be destroyed by fire." I paraphrased Saint Peter, but no one cared about him any longer. The distractions were too great.

A minute later she put down my bill, my credit card, and credit card slip. I guess that was a hint or something. The bar patrons were holding their breath as if I might do something rash. That wasn't my style though. I left her a hundred dollar tip, bent the credit card in half, and put it in my mouth. At first it hurt, cutting the inside of my cheeks, but after a few bites it became easier to gnaw on. I began writing on the pine tree what I had just burned on the napkin. THE SOURCE IS GOD = THE ARROGANCE OF USELESSNESS.

A manager-looking fellow in a light blue button down and paisley tie approached me. "I'm sorry sir, but we're going to have to ask you to leave." He was very apologetic for something that I did. Why were strangers always apologizing for my actions?

I spit out the card on the bar. "Okay, go ahead, ask me." I chuckled at myself. God, I was drunk! What had happened? I was supposed to go rescue Charlie.

"Please leave?"

"I accept your invitation for the outside." I went over to Jumble and gave him the pine tree. "I apologize for making anyone uncomfortable." But I wasn't sorry. The philosophical-theological conversation served its purpose. The bartender got her big tip, Jumble got the respect for being patient and sane in contrast to the buffoon, and the rest got a story to tell at the bar the next day.

The night air rushed into my lungs like a shot of spiked music. Only an evil God would keep humans alive in our condition. We're all diseased in such inconspicuous ways. Blind from syphilis, paralyzed from the waist down from a commercial, delusional from thousands of years of procreation, we hold warts in our genitals from the art on our walls, we laugh out black clouds of phony words from dead men as if there were lessons taught, as if our lungs weren't collapsing, growing tumors for future research, future mouthfuls of dirt, future semen-stained sidewalks, and then we stop thinking that we might be viruses upon the surface of a molecule we call Earth. All these thoughts swirled into the distant sound of a passing train. It felt like steel against steel, the power of perpetual steam, the power of thought, men asking, "Did the wheel or did the human come first?" The answer was as important as the truth. The truth for me, which was simply the next ten minutes, a snooze button for death. The moment perplexed my mind. I could comprehend ten minutes, could find a full bottle of pills, could dig a knife through an artery, could look up into the sky and spot infinity. At that time of the night and that time of the year it was easy to find my way home, even in the most ridiculous circumstances. The moon sat right above my roof, ready to drop down and dip its craters in the dust.

When I got back, I put on my only CD and danced with Mrs. Calypso. "Please, just one dance?" I demanded. "Then I must leave." She was a wonderful dancer. The advertisement wasn't false, so I did not lie to her. Just one song, one dance, and we parted forever. I fell to the floor and became constricted. My body was tight from abuse, scarred skin, dented armor, and a mind of mush. I only could conceptualize nature outside of rationalism, so I went out to the backyard. I puked at the corner of the fence beside the dogwood tree. I guess I was lucky, there weren't any pieces of plastic.

what do you sell your blood for...

Day 12,313

It may have been cloudy, partly cloudy, not a cloud in the sky, but it didn't stop the chance for human greatness, the breaking of the clouds, the possibility of possibility, of ridiculous possibility, of the opportunity to accomplish something real, something past our ego, our fear, our lack of conviction, our arrogance of uselessness. It has crept into our hearts, worms into the apples. All we wanted to do was keep our toes warm, but duty got mixed into a tornado by the hand of a star. Once again I woke up with a grass stained cheek.

I took my supposed expired bus pass and my phone card to the bus stop. I was either going to work or going to call my sister. That way I wouldn't be disappointed. It was just like me to cover my ass like that. The first attempt of possible transport didn't work. The bus driver just shook her head as the beep signifying NO rang from the little distorted scanner. As my feet forgot to turn around, I saw my friend who I tried to give the magic beans. He watched me swipe that card over and over with satisfaction. After giving up, I looked down the aisle at him. He mouthed out, "It's for the best." That really blew me away. I took the three rubber steps back to the sidewalk and watched the bus roll down Central Avenue. As I tried to gain back some confidence before calling Ester, an eighteen-wheeler rumbled to a stop in front of me at the traffic light. Its trailer sides were mirror panels that offered me a hazy reflection of myself. The man looking back at me was filthy, poverty-stricken, beat up, and ragged. I couldn't talk to Ester in this condition. I had to be a man, her older brother, something not to look down upon. I straightened my posture, jogged in place, spit in my hands, rubbed my hands through my hair, and went home. I would come back a new man, an old American, just like them, then wake up the next day, then wake up the next day… then wake up the next day.

After shaving and showering, I found my least filthy shirt and began chugging water. In-between sips I searched for the next charity case, a map of the world, a dead couch, a stereo hanging on by a copper string, a bed that had been replaced by dirt, grass, and insects, some plastic bags, dirty mugs and cups, a pair of dress shoes, *The Rosy Crucifixion*, and that one CD case. That was it! Somehow everything else had managed to disappear. I had cleansed myself. All I needed was a little money to get another bus pass. I could live off my chili until Floyd's real job kicked in, then pay bills and buy more plastic bags over and over until I could look in the mirror and know that the face looking at me was a collector of pawns and guards and prostitutes. Then it hit me. "Charlie?" I hadn't cleansed myself, just forgotten what was behind me. What a fool! I even left the gas can outside that strip mall bar.

My front door was left open, the first fifteen minutes of the walk were forgotten, and this is how it happened again. There was nothing out of my power. My life could just be this same afflicted day happening over and over with God putting in different scenes and characters. I looked desperately for the gas can, but it wasn't anywhere around. After searching the dumpster, the parking lot, and even looking in the front windows as if it would be sitting on a table or something, I saw the manager from the day before. He met me at the door and before I could say anything he pointed behind me, "No sir, turn around!" He said, as if he was angry with me. I barely knew the guy. He had a backup man with him, a cook or a dishwasher, someone dressed all in white.

"Listen, I just want to-"

"No sir, back outside. I will call the police."

The police? Maybe this was my chance to do some hard time in the clink. I would tell the judge that I killed him because he kept calling me *sir* with no respect. It's like someone calling me a *cunt* with a smile and a handshake. "It's my gas can I'm looking for, please, I need it to-"

"We disposed of that before you could do anymore damage."

"What does that mean?" Did he seriously think that I would burn down the bar? Yeah, sure, these thoughts have crossed my mind, but they're just loose ideas that would never tie together.

"Off the property sir, and don't come back."

"Please, it's a matter of life and death." I walked backwards and pleaded my case. "That was my property, this may be your property, but that was mine!" But they didn't care. Nobody cared about shit except saving their own ass. God forbid we give anyone the benefit of the doubt. I left their property and walked toward Charlie. It would be nice just to see her, sit down in the old broken driver's seat, and pretend to drive us into the Pacific Ocean. It was such a great day for a walk anyway. Who could stay angry at the world and its viruses? It was just a little misfortune, nothing that the sight of your abandoned car shining under the clouds couldn't fix.

Even when I saw her from a distance, I couldn't believe she was still there waiting. There was a summer haze under the tires with burning coals and a sadness from clothes that didn't fit any longer. I stretched back on Charlie's hood and stared up into the sky. There was a billboard off to my right. It was a picture of a boy and a girl with hopeless expressions. It read, SAVE A LIFE TODAY. It was for a plasma donation center that was conveniently located just down the road beside a check-cashing store. Crafty advertisements were a dime a dozen, even for such a valiant cause, and especially for the Idiotainical Period. But besides all the cynicism, I actually keep piles of faith in the closet of the omen world, and if lying on one's broken down car and finding the answer up in between a tree and a power line isn't an omen, then I might as well jump on the midnight ghost tonight before the sun sets over all the other billboards of the world. This would have to be the last chance at my new start, and on top of that, I would apparently be saving a life. The evidence of higher powers was adding up.

I walked the six or so blocks down to the plasma donation center. There were two security doors with cameras, buzzers, and bulletproof glass. Were people stealing blood? It would be easier to rob a bank. I pushed through the second door in sequence to the retched buzzer, and then waited to talk to a receptionist. The security issues concerned me. Maybe there was a black market for plasma. Underground doctors performing transfusions and such. Vampires stocking up for the winter.

The receptionist just handed me a novella-sized booklet that I had to fill out, sign, initial, and read, in that order. The waiting area was half-full of people that looked like me in the mirror-paneled truck. I filled out the entire booklet, essentially looking for the part of payment. First time donors received $30. That would have to do. Thirty minutes later I gave back the filled out forms.

"Thank you, now sit down until we call your name."

So I did. I sat by a man about my age, race, and desperateness. The comfort of our similarities drew me to him. I'm sure no one really wanted to talk about why they were there, but I asked anyway. "So, why are you here?"

He cocked his head to get a better look at me. His eyes went into sudden shock along with a humorous curl of his lip. "Well, I'm what they call a humanitarian. I go out of my way, sacrifice to say," He laughed at his rhyming mishap. "To help others. I work at a soup kitchen during my lunch hour, I knit blankets for the homeless, and of course at any chance I get, I donate my extra plasma for poor victims of tragedy, disease, and blah blah blah." He was poking fun at my question, but he didn't know that I was the king of hyperbole.

"I run a literacy program for children, and I also teach adults how to truly be happy in the worst possible moments." I said like I was a twelve-year-old bragging about my new bicycle.

"That's pretty funny." He sounded like he believed me. That was nice. "How about you teach me, because the truth is, I sell my blood for drugs. What do you sell your blood for?" He wanted to be happy in the worst possible situation. I could have told him to just stop worrying about surviving and start focusing on success and money, that possessions and expectations enhance the soul. It seemed to pass the time for most mistakes. But that didn't happen, because his question rattled my brain for the rest of the day. What did I sell my blood for? It killed me that there might be an answer. I was under the impression that I was donating my plasma for a small monetary sum, but that was obviously bullshit. I could sell all the music, books, and furniture I wanted, but once I started selling my blood, well, it was different, very fucking different. "I don't know?" I told the humanitarian about ten minutes later. Then I got up and walked out. I was so lucky to be surrounded by people who teach me every day, teach me how not to be. Most adults stop paying attention to the perverse teaching of other humans, but not me, the ultimate grasper of the obvious. I see a man selling his blood for drugs and I know that it's not a book or a bartender's uniform. Yes, I was very lucky, embracing cancer from overexposure of the moon.

I was walking back home, rubbing the soft jagged scab on my head, listening to my stomach whine, looking out of watery eyes, and fingering through empty pockets. It would have been really easy to just go to bed that night, wake up the next day, and then try again. Give it the old never-give-up attitude! But, I passed by a couple of men sitting against a brick wall in an alley. They were passing a bottle back and forth and it seemed they were complaining about life. The normal person would either turn and forget, or sympathize and work twice as hard from fear of ending up in hobo alley, but not me, not the ultimate grasper of the obvious, no sir. They taught me that the only thing that matters in life is to live. They were alive in an Arcane alley, drinking, and talking about nothing. Perfect examples of living. And at the very least they had each other. I thought about Alex up in New York. Maybe I should go have a beer with him, complain about everything and die the next day.

There were two pay phones up ahead in front of a shoe store. There were about ten people inside the store browsing and such. They already had shoes on their feet yet they were getting more. This baffled me to no end. I picked up the phone and stared into the store like it was a show. After a minute or so a pleasant voice through the receiver told me to "Stop looking into the shoe store and call your sister." So I did. Ester always answered, never my mother. Apparently she had a secret boyfriend, and mom talking to him would be the end of the world. Anyway, it made me laugh to think of the conversation between her and a boy. Maybe she actually repeated things that I told her. That's the kind of thing that makes a big brother sad and happy at the same time.

"Hello?" Her monotone voice said with a touch of expectancy.

"Ester, it's me. I have a few things to tell you, and they need to be fast, and they may be important, or even not so important, it's hard to say, because for one, I don't have a list, so my first point could end up in a ditch somewhere in Montana. Incidentally, how are you?"

There were a couple of heavy breaths. "Pretty good."

"Mom?"

"Pretty good too. She broke her favorite angel figurine, so she isn't too happy right now."

"Tell her that angels only exist in heaven, and heaven is for people who make mistakes. Tell her figurines break."

"Right now?" She asked. I couldn't help but wonder if that was sarcasm.

"Those goddamn figurines. You'd think-"

"Don't say that."

"I'm sorry, it's just that collecting things pisses me off more than anything in the world. If you do anything in life, don't collect things. It'll just make you depressed when you break a figurine, or you have to spend a rare coin to fix something that probably wasn't broken, or part of the collection disappoints you or dies or something. Will you promise me that? Will you?"

"Okay."

"Sometimes I find myself hating you, because you're the only thing in this world that I have to lose. Without you I could really go off the edge, but for now, I don't know? I mean, I'm already waiting on wings of disaster, balancing on some goddamn tightrope, and on one side... on one side is just life, and the other is this chaos. By the way, I'm not calling you a figurine or a stamp or anything. You're just more important than I would hope to make anyone, but what's done is done and we have to live to that tune." Out of nowhere, I began to tear up, but I didn't let it come through in my voice. The big brother had to be strong.

"Okay."

"But beyond all that, you've been listening to these horrible rants for years, since you could understand the word *phony*, but now, now I'm calling you to tell you that your big brother is the phony. I teach you to rebel, to be unique, to not live in fear, to know that the self is all that matters, and I'll get back to that, but for now my point is that just as the normal man is afraid to obey his whims and take real chances with death, I'm afraid to not listen to the ridiculous demands of my brain and take chances with life, so that makes me just as horrible a human as anyone else. But that's going to change soon. I have cleansed myself of just about everything and I'm ready to wake up." I sensed that she had something to say, so I let her regular pause pass and then waited for her response. About thirty seconds passed with nothing, and then all of a sudden that pleasant electronic voice came back. "Time has expired." Then a dial tone replaced the voice.

"God! You son of a bitch!" I yelled into the receiver as if the bastard would hear me better. Some kids passing by repeated what I said. They snickered at their joke. It did sound funny. But I didn't laugh with them. Ester had something important to say and if it took six hours of silence to get it out, I was willing to wait. Those damn omens. Now thinking about the omens, it is possible that they might all be wrong, all so wrong that they smudge together like a slug and a sidewalk. My eyes scanned all the corners of Central and Thomas streets. Sign Guy was nowhere to be found. There had been times when he wasn't there and there wasn't any deep meaning behind it, but this time was different, this time the corners didn't hold his spot, this time a gust of wind didn't hold his magic. I hung up the phone.

I went back home and there was a note on my screen door from Floyd. It had something to do with being near the end of the month and something to do with that damn list Floyd's wife kept talking about. I didn't really know what to make of it. It was vaguely threatening. After writing down Laura's nauseating life philosophy on the back of the note, I pinned it up on my corkboard.

I grabbed a plastic bag and went out to the backyard. It was near the end of the day, but the red ripe tomatoes shone through the shadows. I picked them off carefully as if each one held a piece of my life, and I stared through the thin flesh as if they held a delicate memory that could be crushed at any slight squeeze. When the bag was full, I sat down beside the bare plants and saw the walls of buildings and the city veins intricately flowing down into the soil, all empty and all soon to be dead.

In my closet there was an old rucksack that I'd had since high school. Back then I thought that I was going to join the Army or run off to California or Italy or anywhere except virtually nowhere. The rucksack actually did go out to California to visit Alex. I've got the notebooks to prove it, and the only reason I mention it is because some people don't think Alex really exists, that he's just another hallucination in my world, but those people don't really know the difference between reality and fantasy. Truth is though, notebooks don't prove existence of anyone except the writer, and there is no difference between reality and fantasy. I skimmed over my notes for *The Moron Factory*. It wouldn't make much sense to most.

 I packed up *The Rosy Crucifixion*, almost all of my memories off the wall including Mr. and Mrs. Calypso, an extra pair of socks, and the tomatoes. A head full of dreams and dry feet were the keys to salvation. A crack of thunder came through the walls. I opened the fridge and stared at the bottle of Champagne. I whispered something to myself, and to this day I couldn't tell you what it was. If it were on canvas, it would be a watered-down oil painting of a closed dream. This cryptic message from the devil sat on my mind as I left the fridge open, grabbed my rucksack, and left my home. The sky was condensing together. My hands were filthy, practically black over my palms. Even after clapping and feverishly rubbing them together, only a few sparks of soot drifted off to their destiny, and the rest waited for something bigger. I followed the train tracks and tried to play a game where my feet could only touch the wooden ties. The child is the reborn.

The rain finally came. Just as all situations in which one is dry and they become wet, we have to wonder how we got there. How did these trees cast such long shadows that had now been banished for the last fifteen sunsets? The canopy of a southern summer wasn't to be forgotten or duplicated. I put my hands up in the air and pretended to fly. The reborn shall be cleansed.

For years I have had nightmarish flashbacks where I get run over by a train, my skull gets crushed, my torso gets shredded. It always seemed more like a prophecy than a flashback though. I liked the idea of the two seconds before this possibly happening. There would be phones ringing, buses purring as they waited for the traffic light to change, glass mugs clinking together, passive aggressive laughter, the screeching of metal scraping metal, a desperate air horn that never once saved a life, and the chiseling of an epitaph into stone. All of this within the span of a moment. My dream was those two seconds, and my awakening was the nightmare.

Out of the corner of my eye I saw the first lightning bug of the night. It danced between the raindrops. I looked at my palms and saw that the black dirt had disappeared. I thought of my dad, of my dad's ghost, of all the ghosts swirling around the world, smiling at the absurd skin and bones, complete and unreasonable, linking closed-down train stations, and opening up bolts of air to show us the path. I couldn't wait to fuck up again, I couldn't wait to take one correct step for once, maybe hold my breath like only God knew how, maybe jump into the next boxcar. The huffing ghost train waited for me. It wondered where I was going as I wondered where it came from. I guess the point wasn't to know where I was going. It was illuminatingly strange, sitting there in that boxcar, staring off into the skyline of Arcane. The fading past told me that I hadn't been dreaming, and that all the asinine moments that formed a pile of nothingness in my living room also formed a pile of pages under my bed, and that, just as we all wait for the pinnacle of happiness, I waited for my blood to ripen, and when the train jerked into motion, I turned red, and the city grew smaller, and the steel wheels of the locomotive rolled north, and the nervousness in my stomach was consoled by the sight of my warm breath giving birth to a cloud of steam.

THE END

EPILOGUE

The lady in question, Laura, Floyd's wife, made her way to the backyard. She had known the tenant on the smaller side of the duplex for around a year at that point. When the word *known* is used, in this case, it meant that she knew his face and his words, but it stopped at that. To Laura, the man in question always seemed, a man without consequences, as if he could just arrogantly create life for the most useless reasons. Her concern, idle hands, her reprieve, forgiveness.

She noticed that the tomato plants had been picked. She noticed that the advertisements and letters were piling up underneath his mailbox. Laura knocked on the man's door and then turned the knob. She had not seen the inside of this part of the house in over a year. Her stomach dropped when the cold dark feel of vacancy hit her.

It was virtually empty except for several large items and several small items. The bed, the couch, and the bookshelf made up the former. The latter needed more investigating. Laura peered into the open refrigerator to see the package of rancid ground beef, the empty butter tray, and the bottle of champagne. On the kitchen counter was a set of keys and a record player without records. The bathroom was empty save a dirty towel and a broken mirror. On the wall was a map of Earth and a corkboard with dozens of tacks that now held a single piece of scrap paper. The paper read:

'Just let go of everything and let the waves take you where they will.'

The man next door had left Laura's life philosophy behind. She couldn't recall ever saying this to the man next door, and wondered for a second if he could read her thoughts. If there were anyone she had ever met that could possibly read thoughts, she was sure it would be this man.

On the floor, halfway under the bed and beside a pair of black dress shoes was an unbound manuscript. She gathered up the loose pages and sat on the bed. The title ~~*The Moron Factory*~~ was crossed out and underneath it was scribbled *The Arrogance of Uselessness*. So the lady in question read through the manuscript until finishing the entire farce. Her reaction, confusion, her conclusion, fear.

On the last page the creator of the document had written down in what seemed to be in haste: SEND TO 99 SOUTH 6TH STREET, BROOKLYN NY. With the side note: SORRY ALEX. I DIDN'T KNOW WHAT TO DO. FAITH SEEMS TO HAVE STOPPED WORKING.

Made in the USA
San Bernardino, CA
12 April 2014